The Hot Chocolate Shop

The Hot Chocolate Shop

JENNIFER GRIFFITH

For My Beautiful Sisters in Law—Who Could All be Hair Models

Chapter 1

Roxanna

I had to get this right. Even in the freezing cold, with bare feet on this snowfield. Even though it was something as dumb in real life as making my hair swing in a flat swish, for my job today, it had to be perfect.

I have to be perfect.

"More snap on this take, please, Sanna." Domingo snapped his Spaniard fingers at me to demonstrate. "More twist at the last second, slow and then fast."

"Right." I gave him the go-ahead to roll the camera again. Then, I set my signature enigmatic smile, widened my eyes as much as possible, and swung my waist-length hair.

"That's it." Domingo lowered his camera and gave me one of those marveling looks that I'd grown used to. "Two takes. Wow. They said you were the best, but I wasn't prepared for two takes."

It should've been one.

"Tell me what you need, and I'll do my best to get it on the first try next time." The legendary Fred Astaire prepared for every shoot so that it could be filmed in one take. Fred was my idol.

Someday, if I ever get time, I'd love to watch the scene of Fred tap dancing in the spinning room with someone I love.

At this rate, though—with my shooting schedule for Gloss and the

1

scramble for my master's degree—I'd never have time for dating.

Domingo's assistant called the group together. "We're out of light, so we'll wrap for the evening, but we will start first thing in the morning."

Just prior to sunrise. When the light was best—or right after sundown but before dark. That way, the hazy glow of natural twilight could work its lighting magic without shadows.

Ah, the working hours of my job.

Bitsy raced over to me and placed a warm, fuzzy red blanket over my shoulders. "You were great, Sanna."

"Yes, you were." Domingo packed up his camera. "You impressed me with your professionalism." His eyes twinkled above his gray beard, like a snow field sparkling on a sunny day. "You're going places, young lady."

I couldn't suppress a broad, grateful smile. A tired one. This had been a long day—starting long before pre-dawn light, while hair and makeup staff had transformed me into Sanna.

"Yes, she is." Bitsy hugged me. "Like, back to her room to take a hot bath to be ready for tomorrow." She shuffled me toward the Wilder River Lodge, where I was staying for the week. "He liked that you're such a pro. A word from Domingo could lead to bigger and better jobs, you know. In movies and TV."

Maybe, and it sounded like a dream, but it wasn't the job I wanted. Hair modeling was the most fun I'd ever had, but I needed to focus on my bigger goal—getting that master's degree in English literature pinned down.

"I'm now and always a still-photo model, not an actress." I slipped my feet into the snow boots Bitsy had set out. Heavenly—so warm! "But thanks for your confidence in me."

"You could do anything, I'm sure, Sanna. Why are you back in school?"

Bitsy asked me that question all the time.

"You of all people should know that a job in the modeling business only lasts so long, unless you're a mega-star first like"—I named a few hair- or skin-care models who'd come into the endorsement business after successful television and movie careers. "I'm getting my master's for *after* my Sanna star burns out."

Well, that was only partly true. Having a long-term modeling career would be wonderful. So would acting. I felt so alive in front of the camera. But that was the thing—my life wasn't the right thing to focus on.

Mom's was.

"But you can earn more and more commissions. Just be wise with your income and you can probably retire in five years." Bitsy, as my agent, knew exactly what I earned. But that wasn't the point.

"I like being prepared." Besides, the income had all turned to outgo lately, thanks to Thorn Atkin, my nemesis.

"That is your motto. Always prepared. Like Domingo said, full of professionalism." She laughed. "I think he could have used *perfectionism* instead."

"Normally, that's a hundred percent true." We arrived at the back entrance of the Wilder River Lodge, where I'd be staying for the night. River Tresses was putting me up in the nicest suite with an amazing view of the ski slope-covered mountainside. "But I'm supposed to be going to a local book club tonight, and I'm actually *not* prepared."

"What do you mean, prepared? Are they asking you to speak about your career? Is it a nonfiction-about-careers book group?"

Hardly. "It's something I have to do for grad school. A requirement." For reasons too annoying to explain, I was locked into attending Twelve Slays of Christmas, hosted by Wilder River's Hot Chocolate Shop.

"And you're not prepared? As in …?"

"As in, I"—I winced—"I haven't read the book yet." I shut my eyes and covered my face with my freezing cold hands.

A gasp. "Roxanna! You?" Bitsy stutter-stepped as we reached the outer doors of the lodge. "That's unthinkable!"

Right? "Well, I intend to be totally prepared—by seven o'clock." I looked at the giant clock near the ski-rental door of the resort. "I have three hours. Better crack the spine of the book."

Bitsy shook her head. "You're going to have to read fast."

I hustled to my room and found my copy of Agatha Christie's novel, *Sparkling Cyanide.*

Crime novels. My shoulders bunched. Give me fantasy, sci-fi, historical fiction, biography—all the books. But not crime fiction.

For so many reasons.

I winced as I cracked the spine for the tenth time.

And promptly fell asleep.

My alarm beeped at six thirty—telling me my ride would be downstairs in fifteen minutes to take me to the book group—and I shot up in bed. My heart pounded, and I started hyperventilating.

I shot around the hotel room. There was no time to put my contacts back in. I'd have to wear my thick glasses. My hair looked like ten rats had spent the entirety of my nap turning it into their tangled nest. My makeup was smeared to kingdom come.

With enough vigorous friction to nearly remove skin, I scrubbed my face makeup-free. Otherwise, I'd get arrested for impersonating that creepy clown with the balloon. The alarm beeped again. Five minutes to Danica's arrival.

Danica, my oldest friend and my ride to the Hot Chocolate Shop, was the one person in Wilder River who knew my job status. I'd mentioned that to Bitsy, who'd warned that since I'd already told Danica it was fine—but that it had better not go an inch farther.

Unfortunately I was still only a few pages into the Agatha Christie novel! There wasn't even time to read the Cliff's Notes version of it! I could look up the Wikipedia summary.

That was my only hope.

Oh, mercy. Where was a hat? I dug around in my bag and found something! Aha! A beanie. Baby pink. Not my color. But I shoved my signature waves of dark hair up into it.

How lumpy was it? I leaned toward the mirror, stuffing a stray lock back inside it, and—

Oh, no. The beanie was not only baby pink, it had a cat's face embroidered on it, a gift I'd planned on giving mama-to-be Danica to match the one I had for her baby daughter—with coordinating pink sweaters. Mother-daughter sweaters and beanies. So cute—in theory.

Oh, and let's not ignore the cat ears pointing at the top.

A lumpy cat-head atop my own head.

And I hadn't read the book.

Eighty percent of me whined like a cat in a rainstorm, saying, *Just forget the book club for tonight! Try again another week!* But the stern, logical twenty percent of me shoved her hands on her hips and said, *Suck it up, Dixie cup, and get over there. You have a full twelve of these suckers to attend, whether you like mystery novels or not, or else you can kiss your master's thesis goodbye.*

Fine. Fine! I shoved that stray snarl back into the hat, grabbed the unread book, and headed downstairs.

Glowingly pregnant Danica stomped on the brake as we reached a stop sign. "You didn't read the book?" Her jaw dropped, her eyes widening. "And you're still attending the club? You do know the discussion is being led by Freya, right?"

Winter wind whipped, echoing Danica's horror.

"It's my first time attending. Won't she be lenient?" Ugh, I hated asking for favors, but this book club, Twelve Slays of Christmas, was my one and only option—ugh. Murder mysteries and police and detectives and crime and justice. The muscles in my neck twitched. "You said Wilder River was full of really nice people."

"It's Freya," Danica repeated, as if that explained everything. "If you don't read the book, you're kicked out of the club. I tried joining last spring, during Freya's Spring into Reading session, but I couldn't keep up, thanks to a double enrollment of gymnasts at Candy Cane Cottage."

"And?"

5

"And she didn't give second chances."

Ooh. That didn't bode well.

But—but what choice did I have? It was this or the Russian Literature and Latte group that met weekly in Reedsville. Which would be fine if I weren't working and could read massive tomes all day and night between club meetings.

I leaned my head against the window. One of the cat ears bent, poking into my scalp. I sat up. "What should I do?"

"I don't know, Roxanna. But your hat is cute."

"It's actually for you, and I bought one for your baby."

"It's adorable." Danica rubbed her forehead and pointed across the parking lot to my destination. "You're shivering. Are you cold?"

I was chilled to the bone, despite my cozy nap. From my bag containing Agatha's book, I pulled out the cat sweater and put it on with an apologetic wince. "I bought this for you, to go with the kitty hat."

"It's darling. Meow. You match." She snorted. We pulled into a parking lot with a few cars in it. In front of a cozy-looking building, a large wooden sign read, The Hot Chocolate Shop. "See that truck over there?"

I saw it. An old white truck with yard tool handles sticking up at odd angles from its bed was parked beneath a towering evergreen.

"It belongs to Jeremy's cousin Grant Calhoun."

"That's nice." Wait a second. "I'm not interested in meeting anyone right now."

"He's your type."

I doubted that highly. "I have yet to meet *my type*."

"Then what *is* your type?"

Humph. "I'll know it when I see it." I'd never had time to define it, not since I was too young to know myself well enough. So far, my adult years' experience with men had been wholly disappointing. Okay, that was solely based on Dad's world-shattering lie, but still.

"Well, you'll see your type when you meet him. Girl, he's everybody's type. And not just based on his looks."

6

"I doubt that."

"Trust me, you'll change your mind."

No, I wouldn't. I had a degree to earn and a long-lost dream to accomplish. And a bloodsucking attorney's fees to repay. Much as I wished for it, it was out of the question right now.

"Thanks for the ride and the advice." I gripped Agatha to my chest. "I'll be polite to Jeremy's cousin if I meet him, I promise."

"Good luck with Freya." Danica pulled a scared face. "I can pick you up later. Bye."

I climbed out, and she drove off.

The Hot Chocolate Shop, with its warm, glowing windows, its lone pine tree out front and its soft Christmas-red paint looked welcoming, like Christmas in a box—at least from the outside.

Might as well face Freya and my fate. Someone who owned a place so welcoming had to be forgiving, right?

With a shudder, I climbed the steps to the shop. If I hadn't needed to cover my hair-nest, I would have shaken it out, squared my shoulders, and stalked inside, ready for anything.

Unfortunately, I sported dumb little cat ears, *plus* the fuzzy sweater for Danica. It had two white cats on the front. With the words *Jingle Cats* embroidered on it.

It had looked so cute in the shop when I'd been shooting on location in Japan last year! Now, it just seemed dumb, unless Danica was wearing it and matching her baby.

But I wasn't Danica. And there were no babies on my horizon, more's the pity.

The door jingled, and I entered a heavenly scented room. Chocolate essence swirled in the air all around, as well as warm spices like cinnamon and nutmeg and cloves. Mugs of all sizes and shapes hung from hooks along a pegboard behind the counter. A large glass case contained a display of sandwiches under glass domes that made my mouth water, all on little stoneware plates of different designs. A huge fireplace stood against one side, with chairs and couches nearby, and a fire blazed and crackled.

Wow, talk about a reader's paradise!

"Welcome." A woman stood behind a counter spread with silver kettles. She wore an apron with the name *Freya* embroidered across the front. "Are you here for Twelve Slays?"

"Yes, I'm Roxanna Reid."

Freya checked a list and then looked back at me with narrowed eyes. "So, did you?"

"I'm sorry. *So, did I* what?" I accepted a mug of steaming hot chocolate from her hands. It smelled faintly of almonds. Cute, considering today's club focused on poisoning by cyanide, which smells of almonds.

"Did you read?"

Oh, a pun on my name, Roxanna Reid. Yikes. The moment of truth had attacked much sooner than expected. What to do? Lie? Fall at her feet and beg for mercy? I couldn't.

"Since you're hesitating"—Freya's warm smile faded, and she reached for my mug to take it back—"I'm guessing you didn't."

I gave Freya back the mug, but before we could finalize my dismissal, someone piped up.

"Honesty is the best policy." A man's voice sailed through the air from near the fire.

I walked over to see who had interjected his comment into our conversation. Over a pair of dark-rimmed glasses, a young man with an intelligent aura eyed me.

"Full disclosure, I didn't read the book. No valid excuses either." Something about him made me add a flirtation to my voice. "Did you? Read, that is."

"I take it you like cats."

Cats! Oh, right. The beanie and sweater. "You didn't answer my question."

"You didn't answer mine."

"You didn't ask me a question."

"Yes, I did. I asked if you liked cats."

"No, you asserted your assumption. It's not the same thing. Did you read the book?"

"No, but unlike you, I do have a valid excuse." He lowered the book he was reading—one twice as thick as the murder mystery we'd been assigned for the evening's club—and with a cover and title I recognized. "An excellent one, in fact."

"Oh, yeah?" Excuses bugged me. I rejected them in my own life, and others ought to as well.

"Yep." The guy stood up. He towered over me. At his full height, the breadth of his shoulders became wow-level impressive. If my manager ever saw this guy, she'd ask about signing him to a contract in a hot second.

Speaking of hot, was I standing too close to the hearth? The guy continued to stare me down. It had to be the blazing fireplace. Because I didn't react to ogling men.

Occupational hazard I'd learned to ignore.

Except now, apparently.

I resisted the urge to fan myself.

He's only ogling your weird cat ears and sweater. Not the same as when men gaped while I was a hundred percent hair and makeup, looking like Sanna, the ubiquitous face of Gloss hair products. Right now, I was a cat lady with glasses and lame excuses.

I gathered up my scattered bits of dignity. "I take it you're going to tell me your excuse, er—?"

This must be Jeremy's cousin. The guy with the truck.

Girl, he's everybody's type. And not just based on his looks.

I had major life struggles to focus on right now—regardless of any action-hero magnetism in a hot-nerd package.

"Go ahead. Tell me your excuse." I stood a little closer to him than necessary. "Grant Calhoun." The name rolled across my tongue like a delicious piece of chocolate.

"My reputation precedes me?" He extended his hand.

9

"My friend Danica dropped me off and pointed out your truck. Said you'd be in here."

"Ah. She's great. Glad she married Jeremy. He deserved her." He reached to shake my hand. When our hands touched, my brain emptied, like a can of marbles dumped upside down. "I'm pleased to meet you."

"I'm Roxanna Didn't Read." My voice got scratchy.

He chuckled and simply disconnected our clasp—as if Mr. Eleven-on-a-Ten-Scale hadn't felt any of that electrifying zap.

Dang!

"My excuse is that I'm not a member of the Twelve Slays of Christmas book club. I'm just here to drink Freya's excellent hot chocolate. She owns the shop."

"That is a proper excuse," I reluctantly admitted. The extension cord from whatever source had been lighting me up came unplugged. My voice probably sounded dejected.

Even if I were allowed to attend this club for future "Slays," I wouldn't be seeing this Adonis in flannel.

A few patrons came in, and a couple sat on a sofa facing the fire. The club should start at any moment. I'd better forget about Grant Calhoun—and about joining the club.

"Apparently, I'm just like you: not in Twelve Slays." I tugged at the hem of my cat sweater. Darn cat sweater. No wonder Mr. Everybody's Type felt nothing while I was all plugged-in-Christmas-lights. "I guess I'll come back next week—after reading the book."

"Um ..." He looked over at Freya, who was happily passing out mugs to people who obviously *had* read the Agatha Christie novel.

"Um, what?" I asked.

"If you're not admitted to Freya's club, you're not admitted to the club, period."

What? My throat constricted. "I can't come back?"

His grimace was my answer—and it gibed with what Danica had claimed.

"Seriously?" That was merciless. "No second chances?" I

spluttered, my heart accelerating into criminal-speeding range. "But—"

But I just *had* to be a member of the Twelve Slays of Christmas! It was the only weekly book club on Professor Higgins's *Approved Public Book Club List* within a three-hour radius of my house. The rest met monthly—or were discussing Russian literature. I ask you! How could Russian lit meet weekly? *Anna Karenina* or *War and Peace* in a week's time? Plus, I got hopelessly lost trying to keep track of all the characters' names and nicknames. How could Sasha and Alexi and Alexander and Shuha and Shurik and so on all be the same person?

Normally, I would have said *anything* was better than crime fiction, but not Russian Literature and Latte. Although, that might be my last resort. *Please, please, please, don't make me remember Alexi is Shuha!*

"I really need to be in this group." I pleaded with Grant, as if he were the one making the decision. As if he had power to help me. "Is there anything I can do to change her mind?" We stood near the coat rack by the door, and all the group members were settling into the chairs near the fire.

"Why do you even care? In a book club, other people choose the reading material. Can't you choose your own books?" Grant held up his tome. "Life's too short to read books for pleasure that don't give you pleasure. Don't tell me you only read by assignment."

Unfortunately, when seeking a degree in literature while working full time, that held true.

"Oh, brother." He must have read the truth in my face. "What was the last book you actually *chose* for yourself?"

"A Yardley Gregson sci-fi. You've probably never heard of him." I would've flown through any of Gregson's Captain Vartigan Chronicles and loved every page turn if a book club featuring Gregson had been on Professor Higgins's approved list.

No such luck. And changing her mind would take some kind of Christmas miracle. Higgins had Scrooge written all over her.

"You're kidding." Grant peered at me through his dark-rimmed glasses, his pupils dilating. Oh, fine. I probably imagined that.

"Kidding about what?"

"About Yardley Gregson."

"I mean, it's been a while since I read the series. I'm in school, as you probably figured out. English literature majors don't get to choose their reading material—as you said. But I have the newest one on pre-order. It comes out on Christmas Eve. I'm giving it to myself, and I'll read it when I finish up some other projects. Rewarding myself."

Mr. Everybody's Type stared at me as if I'd beamed down from a starship. "I know it comes out on Christmas Eve."

"All the fans know that. It's been a full year since *Vartigan's Longest Battle*. I heard he is a new dad, and it's taking up a lot of his writing time." His happiness was his fans' agony. "Why look so dumbfounded?"

"I don't know. I just"—he gave my cat garb a once-over—"I pegged you for a witch-with-a-black-cat cozy mystery reader, not a Vartiganian. I'm not sure I believe you."

I ignored the wardrobe slight. And the weird pushback. "It's only the best sci-fi series of all time."

"Prove you've read Gregson." Grant pulled his glasses off, deftly folding them, his eyes wide.

"Why?"

Wow. What eyes they were—and who cared if I sounded like the big bad wolf pretending to be Little Red Riding Hood's grandmother when I noted them? Large and green, with flecks of gold. They were offset by his red flannel shirt. Christmas colors, like gift wrap, but in October.

A gift to me.

It took a second, but I gathered in the wads of torn wrapping paper my attention had become.

"I don't have to prove anything. Gregson is my author crush. I met him at a book signing in Sugarplum Falls last Christmas."

"Not proof enough." He folded his arms over his chest. He was

12

serious about the proof? Why did he care so much?

"Okay, fine, if you're being a book tyrant. In *Princess of Chylock,* I love the scene where Captain Vartigan and the Rygraff Princess are both held prisoner and they have to work together to get out—only to be met by that alien guard with—"

"—with the ten-headed snake." He completed the sentence with me, nodding. "You really are a fan." His eyes narrowed. "Any other sci-fi authors?"

I rattled off a few of the classics—Edgar Rice Burroughs, Jules Verne, Isaac Asimov. "But I read tons of books."

"Just not *Sparkling Cyanide*." Mirth danced in his Christmassy eyes.

"I don't read crime fiction."

"Then why are you so desperate to join the Twelve Slays of Christmas?"

"It's complicated." Nobody should be subjected to my tale of academic woe, let alone someone I'd just met. I pivoted back to my favorite topic. "Have you read Gregson's earlier series, before Captain Vartigan? The one set on *The Endeavor?*"

"You mean the most powerful intergalactic battleship of all time?"

That was the one, and it set off a full five-minute frenzy of discussion of favorite scenes in that series, and two other series by Yardley Gregson.

Grant looked at me like I'd beamed down from *The Endeavor.* "I never would've dreamed I'd meet a fellow freak-fan in the Hot Chocolate Shop in Wilder River."

"Well, I'm not actually living here. I'm in town for a job." One Bitsy had told me to button my lip about. Gloss always insisted on secrecy before launching an ad campaign. They hated copycats.

"I thought you said you were in school."

"It's a freelance thing on the side." Sort of. I had a short-term contract with them, and Bitsy was hoping to make it bigger.

"Gotcha."

"Can you give me a primer on Wilder River? I heard from ... someone—Danica, maybe?—that the river is special. Or its headwaters spring? Used to be a health destination, back in the day?"

The clock struck seven, and Grant didn't get a chance to answer that.

"Welcome, everyone." Freya planted herself in front of the fire and shot glances between Grant and me. "Our Twelve Slays of Christmas discussion starts now."

The other patrons—there were five or six—clapped. Freya shooed us out of the seating area with a sweeping glance.

Grant nodded his head toward the other side of the room, and I followed him. We sat at the bar.

"Dark chocolate or milk chocolate?"

"Both?" I said. "I'm happy with all the chocolate."

He ordered me a mug of hot chocolate with an orange extract add-in. A second later, I was sipping like a queen. "This is the perfect blend of bitterness and sweetness."

"And the orange?"

"Elevates it." I took another sip, the goodness warming me through. Finally! After being so cold all day. "Thank you. But since I'm not in the group, I should have left."

"Well, I had an ulterior motive." He looked both ways. "I needed more time to find out what else you've read."

I could talk about books all day long. It was part of the reason I wanted to finish my master's degree. Not the biggest reason, but a good one.

We talked about fantasy, Tolkien and Sanderson, plus a few others. He'd read those, plus some others that I took notes of. When I was done with school, I'd check them out.

As we talked and sipped our beverages, swirls of steam, citrusy and chocolaty, filled my senses. Not as much as Grant's enthusiasm for books, but also delicious.

"Read any other genres?" I asked. *Please don't launch into*

Russian lit.

"I like pretty much everything." He named a few Greek classics and described them so passionately that it sounded like I'd need to check them out. "It might be unusual, but I really like Victorian authors."

"Like Dickens, you mean?"

"Yes, and Anthony Trollope. And Elizabeth Gaskell." He launched into a passionate verbal essay about the moral lessons in 1870s literature, plus how much an abundance of detail in writing wasn't always a bad thing. "It really draws me into the setting. You can't over-describe the experience of the fox hunt, I say."

Danica was not wrong. Irresistible. His vibe enveloped me. *You had me at "detailed description of riding to hounds."*

Grant Calhoun was *so* my type. And not just because of his broad shoulders and soulful eyes and intensely hot *hot-nerd* vibe.

"How have you read all this stuff? Were you an English major?" That would've made two of us.

"Chemistry," he said in a sultry voice that I probably only imagined.

Chemistry was right. It swirled around in the air like the chocolate essence of the Hot Chocolate Shop.

I had to leave. Right now. Before I forgot all the vital responsibilities of my life—including finding a book club that would accept me.

"Thanks for the chat." I drained the mug, dug around in my purse with a nod, and left some cash on the table. He handed it back to me, and I placed it in my purse. "Danica was right when she told me I'd be glad I met you." Wow, I'd just blabbed. I'd sounded desperate. And I was never desperate.

"Bye!" I dashed toward the door before I could say anything else or do anything unwise, like offer him my number and beg him to call me. Tonight. Keep the chat going.

I'd just placed my hand on the doorknob to leave when Freya

raised her voice.

"Twelve Slays of Christmas almost had a new member tonight." Freya cleared her throat. "Isn't that right, Roxanna Reid?"

I stopped cold. Was she changing her mind? Had she heard Grant's and my book discussion and decided I wasn't a flake about reading after all? "I'm going to really miss out," I said over my shoulder. *Please, let me in!*

Freya stepped toward me. "Since it was her first week in the club and she hadn't been briefed on the normally hard-and-fast rules of our group, I'm considering offering her a chance to stay."

I swung around. If my hair had been free from the cat beanie, it would have swung in a perfect, photogenic arc that sweet old Domingo would've loved.

"Really?" I squeaked in a voice matching the cats I wore. "That would mean the world to me." Elation surged through me. A round of hot chocolate with any add-in for everyone in Wilder River! "Are you giving me a second chance?" Again with the desperation, the begging tone I tried so hard never to reveal.

Freya's stern tone resumed. "My offer is good on one condition." Her head swiveled, hawk-like, and she pinned her gaze on Grant. "Roxanna Reid, you can join Twelve Slays of Christmas *if* you read all the other books before arriving at the book club discussion."

"Of course." Obviously!

Freya wasn't through. "*And* if Grant Calhoun joins."

Chapter 2

Grant

My truck's engine roared.

I should go home. It was late. I'd be tired tomorrow.

My adrenaline pumped far too intensely for me to even consider sleep. Just talking about the novels I'd devoured in less-stressful times made me feel more alive than I'd felt in ages. No way could I sleep. I was floating, soaring, and pulling my jacket's collar up to smell the chocolate that lingered there.

If I were honest, the fiction talk hadn't been the only thing that had made the hairs on my arms rise in goosebumps the size of hailstones in a winter storm.

Roxanna Reid. Talking with Cat-Hat Lady had pumped me so full of helium, I could've been a balloon in the Macy's Thanksgiving Day Parade.

Combined, in normal circumstances, the hat *and* sweater should've been red flags huge enough to not only wave me down but also wrap me up like a gift with a bow.

However … wow. The woman knew her Gregson universe. In fact, she'd respectfully refused to kowtow to my opinions when she disagreed with them, plus she'd offered a few challenging notions of her own. Like the idea that music had been part of Captain Vartigan's problem-solving process, and that his violin-playing freed his mind to work out the perplexities.

Just talking about books—not only the sci-fi books, but others we both loved, like Dickens and Trollope—was like returning home.

Okay, there'd also been that handshake. Great Scott, that handshake!

When our hands touched, it'd been like unlocking an old closet so stuffed full of lost ideas that when it opened, all of them tumbled out on me at once. I'd probably looked like I'd been hit by the Chylockian Beast's stun venom.

Or like a stroke victim.

That was the other reason I was racing back to Wilder Company's lab in the dead of night.

What's special about the river?

The question, loaded with sincere curiosity, had jarred something loose in regard to figuring out the formula. Something that had evaded my grasp for weeks. Months.

The river! It was the key to what I'd been missing in the formula!

I parked crookedly in the nearly empty lot and jogged inside, taking the elevator down to the basement to my new digs in the lab.

"You're here?" Lucy asked as I tore into the room. "It's late. I thought you were trying to get away from here to think." She froze. "Don't tell me. You *thought of it.*"

I tore off my jacket and yanked the clean lab coat off its hanger. "Not all of it, but a portion." Seconds later, I was digging through a storage closet at the back of the laboratory, the light bulb's string swinging so wildly from my violent pull that it hit me in the face.

Kind of like Roxanna, despite the cat hat and sweater.

I'm solidly a dog person.

Roxanna Reid definitely wasn't my type. *Not that your type has done you any favors up to now.*

Ooh, that annoying little voice in my head that sounded like Gandalf resurfaced. Shush!

But he wasn't wrong. Helena. Mom would never forgive Helena

for the wool she'd pulled over everyone's eyes. Or Nessa, the Not-So-Nice. Or Ivory, the worst of the lot, who had plastered my name all over her social media feeds after our breakup and then created a holiday breakup song highlighting my weaknesses to catapult herself to fame.

For someone as level-headed as you, you sure do fall hard. Gandalf's voice crackled at me like a bad AM radio connection.

Well, that had been true in the past, but I wouldn't be falling hard for Roxanna Reid, who didn't read the assignment. Nope. Double nope. Especially since I might not see her again—since I'd told Freya unequivocally, no. I didn't have time to be in her cocoa and crime book club.

Freya was just being a busybody. And she had no right.

What did Roxanna want with the book club, anyway? She was only visiting from out of town, working a freelance job. Why bother? Especially when she was in school?

Where was she from? I hadn't asked the usual small-talk questions. But somehow, I already had a sense that I knew her better than any of the women I'd dated for weeks or months in the past.

Frankly, I'd basically sat slack-jawed while she listed her favorite scenes between Vartigan and the Rygraff Queen, and while she did so, a scene had played out like a movie in my mind of Cat Lady playing catch in the snow on Christmas morning with Dasher, my golden retriever.

When her conversation needed a response, I'd snapped back to attention—tearing my eyes off the luscious fullness of her lower lip.

The Rygraff Queen was known intergalactically for her full-pout lower lip.

If there were a movie of the Vartigan Chronicles, Roxanna could audition. The rest of her appearance could be enhanced to make her as gorgeous as the queen, but …

But then Roxanna would use those full lips to kiss whoever was the leading man.

What was I thinking?

Geez. Good thing I opted out of the book club. Twelve Slays of Christmas? I'd be slain in one slash of seeing Roxanna again. And then I'd be left bleeding on the ground by a pout-lipped woman.

Again.

"Found it!" I laid hands on the clear plastic bottle labeled *De-ionized—Source, WRS,* and a date from far too long ago, but it might still work.

Straight from the headwaters spring upstream from Wilder River, source waters of the mighty river, this was perfect! Just what the formula lacked. Well, at least one thing. Wilder River springs water had been part of the original formula years earlier by River Tresses.

How did I know, when I'd only been working in this lab for a year? I'd been a reader of all things—including the labels of hair products in my bathtub—when I was growing up. Mom loved River Tresses. She used to have a full head of red hair, her crowning glory, she'd called it with good humor—and then said, *Other than you, Grant.*

Still made me all warm inside, despite all she'd lost recently.

The energy that had been unleashed by talking about books with Roxanna still circulated through the channels of my brain. Ideas sparked left and right. I raced around the room, collecting equipment and gathering ingredients for the formula for the newest River Tresses shampoo—the one that would level up the company and put the plant that employed half the town on solid footing for the decade to come.

It just *had* to.

Measure, pour, stir. Heat, cool, test.

Beads of perspiration formed on my forehead.

River Tresses desperately needed a larger market share—tricky for a little David-like company against hair-care Goliaths like Gloss.

The problem was that no matter what formula I tried, nothing quite hit the mark.

"Results?" Lucy asked, hovering and making me jump.

"Were you working here when they used to use water straight from the Wilder River as an ingredient?"

"Before my time." Lucy lifted the bottle. "Wilder River-sourced de-ionized water. Interesting." She set it down. "You want a cookie?" One of the famous Calhoun pumpkin spice chocolate chip cookies waved in front of my face, trailing cinnamon, nutmeg, and clove scents. "It's great-grandma's recipe."

"Really?" I stepped away from the Bunsen burner. "Food in the lab?"

She chomped down on a bite, her gray bun bouncing. "Yup." She chewed merrily. "You should try them. I baked them this morning. They're fresh." She held a cookie close to my mouth, and I took a sweet bite of the pumpkin-spice goodness. "There, that's better. You're here late and probably missed dinner."

"And cookies are a substitute?"

"Good enough." Her cherubic cheeks proved she'd used the sweet standby often. "Don't feel bad about missing the mark with the formula attempts. Every mistake takes us closer to the actual solution— something true in many aspects of life. Including dating."

Not this topic again. She might be my late father's first cousin, but Lucy was only my coworker, not my dating coach. "Remember last time? *Ivory.*"

"Ivory." She hummed the melody of the awful song Ivory had recorded last Christmas—the one that had lyrics featuring what a disappointment I'd been as a gift from Santa Claus, and why she was dumping me on Christmas Eve.

It'd gone viral.

Ivory was a viral virus, as far as we were concerned.

"No more dating beautiful, heartless women." I was done with gorgeous women. Ivory's "No Nerds for Christmas" song had sealed that door shut.

Maybe I should've revealed my sci-fi-loving, science-fascinated side to Ivory first thing when we'd met. Of course, I'd been working as the plant manager at the time, and she'd only seen me as a guy on the fast-track to becoming C.E.O. of River Tresses.

When I'd dropped the bomb that I was leaving my prestigious leadership position to work in the lab, she gave me a death stare. I learned we were through when she sent me a link to the video of her song.

It should've been aimed solely at me. Not the whole world of women who'd considered themselves betrayed by secret-nerds.

Which all came back to my point: I didn't trust women who threw themselves at me. Roxanna Reid had thrown herself at me like a wrapped gift of sci-fi-obsessed mania—with a huge heave-ho-ho-ho.

Danica was right. I'm glad I met you.

Nope. I shoved the words from my mind. And Gandalf's pesky nudge to respond with, *Same here.*

So, even if Roxanna Reid's big, brown baby-deer eyes hadn't been connected to the cat-hat-and-cat-sweater ensemble, I would've said no to their pleading about the book club.

Burn me once, shame on you. Burn me countless times? Might as well have me on a spit over a Bunsen burner, ladies.

Forget that.

Ouch, my burned fingertip still stung as a reminder.

All of which was why I told Freya—and Roxanna—no Twelve Slays of Christmas for me.

Chapter 3

Roxanna

Danica met me for brunch on Friday morning at the Wilder River Lodge. "You met Grant, I take it?" I'd caught an Uber back to my hotel room the previous night, so we hadn't talked.

"How could you call him everybody's type?" Total misrepresentation. "Dude is his own type, and no one else's." Self-absorbed nerd was how I'd finally labeled him after stomping back and forth in my room at the Wilder River Lodge last night.

An incredibly chemistry-laden, self-absorbed nerd, but still. I fanned myself for a split second, before I recalled again how he'd tossed aside my one and only chance at making progress toward my master's degree as if he were throwing an apple core out the window of his car, while yelling *Biodegradable!*

Danica set down her fork with its bite of waffle still loaded. "Are you sure we're talking about the same Grant?"

"Tall, dark, strapping, impossibly handsome, wears glasses?" I left out the part about the Christmas present color combo of his eyes and the red sweater. "That Grant? Haven't you ever noticed he's also a self-absorbed nerd?"

"Well, I've known him practically my whole life, and no. Never once. He spends his weekends helping his widowed mom. He was valedictorian, an all-American athlete, and was the youngest manager at the plant. The town hero, more or less. The opposite of nerd."

Whoa, and Danica hadn't even mentioned how well-read he was. Or that he got passionate about the moral lessons in the writings of a Victorian author. Or that he'd studied chemistry and exuded it from his pores too. "I repeat, *not my type.*"

"Please." Danica rolled her eyes. "He's just like you, Roxanna Reid."

"I hope not!"

"I mean, you're every man's dream girl."

Tchuh. Hardly. That was ridiculous. Besides, I wasn't the topic right now. "The point is, I got ejected from the book club."

"Because you hadn't read the book? I warned you about Freya's strict rules."

"Actually, no. She was willing to overlook that. Freya booted me solely thanks to Grant Calhoun."

Danica snorfled. "What? Did you two insanely attractive people find each other instantly irresistible and commit a public display of affection?"

"Ugh. Stop. More like I wanted to commit a public display of *dis*affection. Humph."

With some coaxing, I explained the setup Freya offered and Grant's *hard no* response.

"That's actually shocking. That's not the Grant I know."

"Well, that's the Grant I know." I could have started crying on the spot when he'd given me a look of disgust, like I was reindeer road-kill, and marched out of the Hot Chocolate Shop. "Everything about getting this master's degree is roadblock after roadblock, Danica. I guess my only option now is to read Russian literature every waking moment."

"What's that supposed to mean?" Danica finally took a bite of her Belgian waffle. "What does Russian literature have to do with Grant?"

"It means, in short, I get to postpone my graduate committee even looking at my master's thesis by almost a year and a half, since I can't be in Twelve Slays of Christmas."

I looked out the window at the beautiful, snow-covered ski slope I'd spent all morning traipsing, as a frostbite lab experiment, minus the scientists.

Ugh. Science types.

"I'm not letting you blame Grant unless I know the details. What's with the Russian lit, Roxanna?"

"You're right. This isn't technically all Grant's fault. Truthfully, I shouldn't blame anyone but myself. Well, *and* Dr. Higgins."

"Dr. Higgins!" Danica pushed back in her chair and laughed. "Back in college, every time my roommates and I said her name aloud, we chased it with the mean song Eliza Doolittle sang about wanting revenge on 'enrietta 'iggins." She sang a few bars. Danica shoved a big bite of waffle in her mouth and spoke through it. "Can't you change cooperating professors? Request a new committee?"

Tried. Failed. It turns out she'd made a special request to the department that I be assigned to her. They granted her request, not mine.

"Thanks for meeting up, Danica." It was time to head back to Reedsville. My car provided by Gloss would be out front soon.

Danica left the tip, and I paid the bill. "Did you say you're working in Wilder River now?"

"No, my assignment here is finished. I was only planning on coming up to Wilder River for the book club." The photo shoot had been a one-off. Bummer, since working with Domingo had been great, a real privilege. "I don't know when I'll be back."

"Oh," Danica gave me one of those exhausted smiles. "If I go to Reedsville for shopping, we should meet up at Bread and Breakfast."

"Be sure to invite me to the baby shower." I hugged her, and she left.

Upstairs, I gathered my things, and then I checked out of my room and went out front to meet the car Gloss had hired for me. The two-hour drive gave me a chance to continue reading Agatha Christie all the way

25

down the mountainside, back to Reedsville. No relation to me, Roxanna Reid. Different spelling.

I snapped the book shut on the second-to-last chapter.

Giving up on my master's degree wasn't an option.

There had to be a solution to this quandary!

"Driver, take me to campus instead of my apartment, would you?"

A few minutes later, I stood before Dr. Henrietta Higgins in as contrite a pose as possible.

"Would you consider adjusting your requirements about the book club?"

"No."

So she wouldn't even hear me out? "I am asking you to allow me to start my own weekly book club." Without Twelve Slays of Christmas as an option. Desperate times, right?

"We have been over this." She huffed an annoyed sigh. "My requirements are not negotiable, Miss Reid."

At least she hadn't called me Sanna. Once, she'd slipped up during class and used my professional nickname in front of all the other students, and she'd added an eye roll. The class members had smirked in my general direction. Well, the women had. Weird and slightly ungrateful of them, since they all seemed to buy Gloss products.

"A change of circumstances has derailed my progress, and it might take almost a year now." Instead of the twelve-week plan I'd had in mind.

She held up her palm. "The requirement was and remains this: that you attend an approved public book club twelve times. While there, you will exchange opinions and reflections with a diverse set of readers. You will learn firsthand that literature creates a bond between unalike humans."

What if I already knew that extremely well after a too-brief conversation with Grant Zero Calhoun?

"This skill is absolutely *vital* for leading literary discovery in a college classroom setting."

"And I am good with that, but Dr. Higgins?"

"Sanna?" It dripped with mockery.

Urgh. "In the meantime, as I develop this vital skill set, could you at least examine my research proposal? Then, by the time I'm finished with the book club"—which had to get underway somehow—"I'll be ready to jump right into research."

"No." She looked down at a stack of handwritten essays. Dr. Higgins required all essays to be handwritten *during* her class period. No time to mentally prepare.

Which meant I'd always had to over-prepare for her classes, a serious drain on my mental resources.

Twelve months was a long time. During that year, I'd be paying tuition to remain enrolled in the graduate school. That massive chunk-o'-change outlay would set me back yet again from my other, years-long financial priority: repaying Dad's ridiculous legal fees to Thorn Atkins.

"Well, perhaps you have recommendations for weekly book clubs besides those featured on your current list?"

"The list stands, Sanna."

I ignored the disdain. "As you know, the only weekly club I can find on it, besides the one in Wilder River, two hours away, is Russian Literature and Latte."

"It's a quality group." The Oppressor's smile showed her back teeth. Were they sharp-pointed, or was I imagining it? "Russian Literature and Latte meets at Dr. Ulvane's home tomorrow night."

Higgins looked at her well-chewed fingernails. "But like many clubs, reading the selection ahead of time is *required.*"

Don't remind me. My failure still stung in the light of day. Almost as much as Grant's rejection.

"And I doubt even *you* would have time to complete *Anna Karenina* by tomorrow night."

So she *was* aware of my normal tendency to show up to things highly prepared. Why sneer at it?

"I have read *Anna Karenina*, actually. In the tenth grade." Though not as an assignment. I'd just liked the portrait the publisher chose for the front cover and checked it out of the library. "It's a long book. You're right. But I'm prepared."

I could do this. I steeled myself with a breath. Twelve Russian novels in twelve weeks? Sure. I was Roxanna Reid. I *did* read.

My little balloon of hope soared.

"You've read it." Higgins's upper lip curled for a second, and then came the serene superiority as she looked down her nose from above her pince-nez. "If it was during your tenth-grade year, you obviously haven't reveled in the translation by Walpole released last year, which *our* group is discussing at length."

Our group? I stifled the gasp. Higgins belonged to Russian Literature and Latte?

Bile climbed up my throat. "It's still the same story."

"Not remotely! Walpole's excels all other translations," Higgins went on, extolling its virtues. "For instance, instead of saying, 'Every unhappy family is unhappy in its own way,' it makes the subtle, but arguably *earth-shattering* adjustment to, 'Every unhappy family is unique.'"

At least the adjective *shattering* was accurate. *Meaning-shattering* and *poetic-grace-shattering*, more like. No way could I attend Russian Literature and Latte with Higgins and her Walpole-translation-worshipping friends. Er, fiends.

Grief. "Well, if Walpole is the required for tomorrow's discussion, I'd better join a different *weekly* club." I hung on the word *weekly*.

"Don't try to rush your way through this assignment, Miss Reid." She frown-smiled at the futility of my efforts.

Get a new cooperating professor, everyone had said, including Danica, earlier today. Oh, I'd tried. And failed. Higgins had gone to the dean and specifically requested me.

I'd argued, presented hefty cases to the administration, and been denied the switch.

None of which had sweetened Higgins's feelings toward me, as it turned out.

Shocker.

I slouched out of her office to sit under a tree and weigh my distasteful options.

If only I could just keep my current job forever. It was fun. But that was so impractical. I had to prepare for the future, and Mom's legacy lit the way. I'd be stupid not to follow that lamp for my feet.

Outside on the bench under the leafless tree, I gazed up at the snow-covered mountains in the direction of Wilder River. They already had snow, and Reedsville would soon.

I pulled my hair out of its french braid and shook it out. I'd *wash that professor right out of my hair*—somehow.

My phone played the theme song for Captain Vartigan's biggest nemesis, the Chylockian Beast.

Great. The other person I needed to wash right out of my hair.

With a hefty cringe, I answered. "Mr. Atkins." I couldn't call him Thorn, or I might add the *In My Side* part of his name.

"Your monthly installment is overdue, Sanna." Thorn Atkins, Reedsville's worst attorney, sneered through the phone. "Payment is due immediately."

"Thanks for the reminder, Mr. Atkins." Blast Thorn Atkins for not only losing Dad's embezzlement case but for also requiring Dad to pay attorney's fees for the plaintiffs as well.

And blast Dad, while we were at it. *Sorry, Dad. Mom may have loved you to distraction, but you didn't deserve her.*

"I'll get that check over to you this afternoon." He always required cashier's checks.

"No check today. I'll want cash."

"Cash!"

"Unless you have gold pieces, that is."

"Gold pieces," I deadpanned. "For your dragon's lair."

"Don't think of it that way. Think of it as you're St. Nick, and you throw them down the chimney of my house on Christmas Eve and they land in my children's stockings."

"You don't have children."

He yukked out a laugh. "Of course I don't!" Another yuk-yuk. "I'm taking that gold and hitting Waikiki for the holidays, watching all the bikinis go by. The true meaning of Mele Kalikimaka."

Somebody stop me from wishing him the worst Christmas ever. "So, you're saying I don't need to pay you until Christmas Eve, since I'm apparently your own personal St. Nicholas with gold pieces."

"I wasn't saying that, Sanna."

"I'd prefer if you called me Miss Reid during business dealings."

"I thought you dropped your last name so you wouldn't have to be associated with your felon father."

"That felon was your client, Mr. Atkins." *And you failed him. And me. And justice itself.* Thorn Atkins, world's worst lawyer. I hung up—before I said anything else, like reverting to my original, naïve stance on my father's innocence.

I headed to the bank, where I withdrew the largest amount of cash they allowed—draining my checking, as well as my savings.

There went next month's rent.

What was I going to do? I'd have to give up my apartment in Reedsville at this rate. And to think—Bitsy considered my life one of stashing away savings for the future.

If only.

If only I didn't have to deliver the payment in person, too. But I did, walking briskly inside the dreaded law firm, next door to the dreaded bank, which only served as a funnel for all my earnings.

"This is for Mr. Atkins." I crumpled the edges of the envelope in my grip.

"Which one?" The teller looked at me with big, vacant eyes, as if she had no idea she was working for the enemy yet. "Older or younger?"

The front desk person, a rotating identity, always asked this, so I

30

should've specified. "Younger." The one with the moral bankruptcy case pending in all courts in the world. "Thorn," I gave her a sickly smile.

"You're Sanna." Her vacant eyes took up a tenant. "I use Gloss just because of you, you know. Do you really use the products? Your hair is even shinier in real life."

"Thanks." The sweet words actually softened me. "I really love it. And they let me try all the new products."

She looked back and forth furtively, and then spoke in a quiet, conspiratorial tone. "Are there new products coming out soon?"

I'd heard rumors that the research team had scrapped all recent ideas and they were now looking for the Next Big Thing. "I can't confirm or deny," I said, which was a hundred percent true, "but watch for something around Christmastime." That'd been all Gordon Gloss, the CEO of Gloss, had hinted at during his last press conference.

New products were always fun. Would they pick me to showcase them? If only!

"Thanks, Sanna." She fluffed the sides of her hair. "You are even nice in person. I'm sorry you have to pay Thorn any money. I'm sure you can afford it, though."

Sure, if I counted the fact that I'd sold Dad's house to pay the *other* lawyer off first, and was now shoveling all my income at Thorn the Object of Scorn.

"You can go right back and see him. He's not doing anything right now."

Shocker. I'd be surprised if he was doing anything ever. He'd done nothing for Dad.

I walked in, smacked the fat envelope of twenties down on Thorn's desk, and turned away before the man in the brown suit and too-wide tie could insult me.

One of these days, I'd be done with Thorn. And with Dad's trust-wrecking past. And with Dad altogether, if I could help it.

Grandma wouldn't like that, but still. Her daughter had loved

31

Dad—and Dad hadn't loved me enough to keep his integrity intact. Shouldn't that be a bare minimum expectation?

"Have you gone to visit your dad in prison?" Thorn's words froze my steps in mid-air. "I heard you haven't."

Who did Thorn Atkins think he was, Grandma? "Thank you for the suggestion." I closed Thorn's door behind me.

He was not Grandma.

You should go visit him in prison, Grandma's voice whispered, as if summoned by Thorn Atkins.

I flicked her advice into a trash can full of shredded documents as I passed by.

Outside, the air was at least fresh, if freezing and hinting of snow with its iron-fresh faint dampness. I walked a few blocks with a mantra going. *Now what am I going to do?*

No weekly *approved* book club existed except the Russian one—all full of Dr. Higgins and her smug intellectualism.

Well, there was the Twelve Slays of Christmas book club. But that was off the table, thanks to Freya's intransigence and Good-Looking Grant's jerkitude.

There had to be a solution. Didn't there?

I needed to think. Or not think, as was a better problem-solving method for me. Reading would help.

I plunked down on a bench beneath a tree and from my purse pulled out a copy of *Forfeit,* the Dick Francis novel Freya had assigned for the following Thursday. I'd finished *Sparkling Cyanide* on the ride back to Reedsville, and I'd bit back the sour taste of the whole *bringing criminals to justice* theme.

Agatha Christie's book had been good. Dick Francis was good so far. I'd read the first chapter of the novel. Good writing, captivating character, Tyrone. I was into it.

Besides, I should try to be prepared for *all* contingencies. Freya might soften, right?

Ha. But hope sprang eternal.

I read until my phone rang. "What's up, Bitsy?"

"Roxanna, where are you? Can you come to my office? I'll send a car."

Chapter 4

Grant

I finished adjusting the lights on Mom's house. She wanted them up before the big Calhoun family Christmas celebration—and by *before*, she meant several *weeks* before. Based on the number of Tupperware containers of pumpkin cookies already cramming her freezer, she expected a crowd.

Well, the Calhouns were a crowd. Dad's family knew how to party—and by party, they meant *eat until they could barely walk and do some dignity-defying karaoke even though they didn't drink.*

"The lights are up." I bit into an apple I'd harvested from Mom's Granny Smith tree last month. Sour. Ouch, it activated my salivary glands. "They're all working, I checked."

"Speaking of working, that's what you're always doing these days. Remember when you used to be in management and had weekends off?"

I remembered. "There's some big stuff coming up." No one had announced it, but I'd seen the numbers and how they trended even a year ago, when I was upstairs with the bigwigs. Something had to change at River Tresses, and for whatever reason, I knew in my heart that responsibility fell squarely on the shoulders of the great-grandson of Richard Grant Wilder. They hadn't named me after him for nothing.

"How about doing something fun for a change? Read a book or

something." She aimed a thumb over her shoulder at the wall-length bookcase, unwittingly gouging my guilty, sore-spot. "You spent enough of your old management salary on all those. Now, they're just collecting dust."

"You could read them, Mom." Gregson and Tolkien and Trollope all blinked at me from the shelf—accusing me of talking about them but not going back to their wells of wisdom.

Roxanna Reid loved reading.

"Me? Read?" She guffawed. "And miss Richard Dawson and Wink Martindale?"

Mom was right. There were too many game shows to watch to waste time *reading*. Plus, she liked handwork, and she could do that while she watched but not while reading, so I couldn't fault her. She'd made a lot of colorful afghans and scarves for the Calhoun extended family over the years.

She was quirky, but she was Mom, my mom, and I'd do anything for her. She'd given a lot for me to get where I was, especially after Dad died when I was too young to remember him. I owed her all the respect, whether or not she approved of my sci-fi novel-hoarding.

"I'm not all work." I sat down on the arm of the velvet, brown-and-yellow-flowered sofa. "I do fun stuff. I went to one of those book clubs Freya Wilhelm sponsors at the Hot Chocolate Shop." Did it count? All I'd done was drink the hot chocolate and talk to … Roxanna.

"Shoppe, you mean." Mom pronounced it *shop-pee*. "I'll never forgive her for leaving off the *pee*, you know."

Poor Freya. "All she did was spell it right on the sign she ordered."

"She married the Wilhelms' eternal bachelor school teacher son and then acted like she knew better than all us Wilder River folks by fixing our spelling preferences." Mom crossed her arms over her chest, skewing the little Santa-hat-wearing cat's face on her house-coat.

Santa Cat. Roxanna had worn one of those. Or was it three?

Criminy. The Cat Hat woman had taken up residence in my mind without my permission. A squatter!

"Worse, I heard she's not even making the little ham sandwiches anymore." Mom's complaint brought me back to earth and the Hot Chocolate Shop.

"Freya still makes ham sandwiches, Mom." I averted my gaze from the cat's face on Mom's housecoat. It was making me squirm—why?

"Ham sandwiches should not contain Swiss cheese and be served on sweet Hawaiian rolls drenched in butter."

If I waited, maybe Mom would process her own words and realize how good that sandwich actually sounded. Freya's hot Hawaiian ham sliders made the old sandwiches from the place look like dry, crumbly shadows of the current delicious offering.

Fat chance when Mom had dug in her heels. "Nor should they be served hot!" She harrumphed. Her knitting needle pointed skyward in defiance. "I'm not budging. She needs to go back to the original sandwiches. And to the shop-pe."

"Mom. You haven't even tasted them."

"Don't need to. They're probably overpriced."

They weren't. "If I bring you one, will you try it?"

"Nope." Mom pointed the needle at my chest. "Unless you consider getting out of that mad scientist mode and going back to being in charge at the plant. Where you belong. They need you, Grant."

They needed me in the lab. "I'll think about it." *For one second and then reject the idea.* Did I miss being in the management track? Sure. I had a knack for leadership, and I actually missed the people more than the responsibility.

But someone had to take charge of getting River Tresses out of our product-development slump. Gloss was beating us by an exponential margin.

"I think I'll make myself a ham sandwich." I got up and went to Mom's kitchen. She didn't have any Hawaiian rolls, but there was some Wonder Bread. Where was the mustard? I hunted in the fridge. No ham. No mustard.

I settled for peanut butter and honey.

Roxanna Reid smelled like honey. Gandalf showed up again. *You're eating that sandwich because you are trying to relive the essence of Roxanna.*

Please!

You knew there was no ham in the fridge.

Fine, ham was never in the fridge at Mom's house except right after Easter and Christmas.

A Christmas song popped into my mind, the one with chestnuts roasting, and there I sat with Roxanna, at the fire, warming our hands. She shared the last bit of ham from her sandwich with Dasher, and then rested her head on my shoulder, while bells jingled in the distance …

What was it about Roxanna that seemed to make me think repeatedly of holidays and warmth and home?

I went back into the living room with my sandwich wrapped in a paper towel.

Mom's knitting needles dropped to her lap. "I did hear the sandwiches there were sweet *and* savory." She had a notorious sweet tooth.

"Freya makes her own Hawaiian rolls with honey as the sweetener. The honey is sourced locally, so it's reminiscent of the wildflowers around Wilder River's mountains. Plus, it's good for any local allergies." Not that Mom had allergies, but she did love talking about health, especially health fads, and not just game shows. In fact, Mom's health-conscious conversations were probably the main driver for my attempts to save Wilder River through improving the health-improving aspects of the River Tresses products.

Thanks, Mom.

Mom had perked up a lot and said, "Honey is pretty miraculous stuff. You know they've used it not just as a sweetener but also on wounds? For millennia …" She went into an explanation, and she even included a few anecdotes from her extended family, where a second cousin had been bitten by a poisonous spider. The bite just wouldn't heal—until her cousin's wife daubed it with honey. "I think it was a special honey from Mexico."

I took a bite of my peanut butter sandwich with the honey essence. Not special from Mexico, but it did remind me of Roxanna.

Suddenly, an overwhelming wave of shame toppled my pride. I put my sandwich down, my mouth completely dry.

Roxanna needed me—needed nobody but me. And I let her down.

Chapter 5

Roxanna

Bitsy's office was bright, decorated with huge pictures of me—swinging my hair or running my fingers through it, or letting it fall over one of my heavily made-up eyes.

Since I was her biggest client, it made sense, even if shock hit me every time.

Frankly, with her commission on my salary, Bitsy didn't need other clients. Which always struck me with the horror of just how high Thorn's outstanding fees were.

"Sanna!" She only called me that when she had official news about my modeling jobs. She came over and offered me a cold water bottle. "Domingo already touched up the photos from yesterday's shoot, and the execs at Gloss want you to do another shoot."

"Thanks." I unscrewed the cap and sipped the water. "What's new about that? They always schedule their upcoming shoots right after finishing one."

"Ah, but this is a filmed commercial, not photographs for a print layout."

"Filmed?" My chin dropped and my eyes flew wide. "As in, I'd be acting, not just modeling?"

I didn't act. Of course, teaching was kind of like acting, so I'd have to act if I ever got put out to modeling pasture and switched over to my

Plan B career of teaching literature at a college level. My wise, practical dream.

Yes, a film contract would put me one giant step closer to paying off Thorn Atkins, but that would delay (again) my book club requirement for Dr. Higgins.

It tore me in two.

"Where is the job?" I sat down on her plush sofa, slipped off my shoes, and tucked my feet up under me. "When would I start?"

"That's just it. The execs loved yesterday's location so much, they want you to go back to Wilder River for filming." Bitsy's voice was tight. Something about it bothered her, clearly.

"It's very beautiful," I agreed, probing her face for any clue to her hesitation. "What's wrong?"

She pasted on a smile. "So you'll do it? They're offering to put you up in the lodge every week."

"Wilder River Lodge?" The lodge at the ski resort was posh stuff with plenty of amenities, including the view and the amazingly comfortable bed. *Which was my downfall. It'd made me sleep when I should've been awake reading.* "And what do you mean, every week?"

"Yep. Lucky you! Domingo insisted it be you. Don't worry. You'll have plenty of backup help, since this is a new type of gig. I'll come be your assistant."

"Thank you!"

Bitsy grinned, but then her face fell. "Oh, I forgot. Marseille has her dance camp all this month. I can't miss that." Her little daughter came first. Which made sense. "They're practicing for the Nutcracker. I think she'll get a spot in the Reedsville Ballet's performance, if she learns the part well enough. Might even be Clara."

That was a stretch, since Marseille was only seven, but a mother's heart never faltered.

"I hope she gets a wonderful role."

"Me, too, but it would mean I couldn't be there with you weekly."

"Weekly?" I asked again. "What's this *weekly* thing?"

"They're planning a dozen different commercials, one per week until Christmas. All in Wilder River." Again, Bitsy looked pained.

The twelve shoots of Christmas. Freya would get a little chuckle from that. However, being there every week would cut out even the Russian literature club, if I was assigned to be in Wilder River until Christmas. "Wilder River?" How could I help but consider it a dead end on the road to my master's degree goal? I chugged water to process the situation.

"I know you. You drink water like that when you're having doubts." Bitsy put on her tough-agent hat. "Do you want this job or not?"

Splutter! "I want it." *I want Thorn Atkins out of my life.* And the chance to actually *act* instead of stand still or spin? When would that ever come my way again if I pushed against Domingo, my Spaniard cheerleader? He was behind this, for sure.

"So, what's the glugging down water? It should be an obvious yes, signing on the line this instant."

"There's just someone I'd rather not run into." I *didn't* want to be in the same town with Grant Calhoun, with the danger of running into him and perhaps incurring an assault charge. Or at least an *insult* charge.

"Shouldn't be a problem." She held up a contract and pointed to a highlighted section. "Sanna won't be running into *anyone.* If you go out, it's going to be incognito. Right there in the NDA from Gordon Gloss."

Gloss and their NDA obsession.

I homed in on Bitsy's nervous glances to the right and her uneasy frown. "There's something you don't like about this, Bitsy. Tell me what it is."

"Me? No. Nothing. No problem. I love this. You're already my biggest client."

"You can't tell a lie to save your life, Bitsy." It made her a terrible agent for other models but the perfect agent for me. Liars were not

41

welcome.

"I don't know. I have a good imagination. Probably listening to too many crime podcasts. If I get more evidence than just my own weirdness, I'll talk to you about it."

"I'll hold you to that." Meanwhile, should I sign? If it meant hiding out from Grant Calhoun and postponing the book club requirement *again*?

"Is it a yes, then?" Bitsy held out the paperwork.

"I don't know! It comes back to that book club thing!"

"I thought you joined a book club in Wilder River. Shouldn't this make your life easier?"

"It didn't work out." Heated fury raced through my veins again. "And, before you ask, I'm not allowed to form my own club. Or join twelve separate ones to attend all at once. Or change cooperating professors."

"Online?"

I shook my head. Dr. Higgins always claimed online book clubs were fake.

"The Paleozoic age called. They want their professor back." Bitsy sprang a '90s joke on me.

"None of the obvious or creative solutions apply." I was stuck in a twelve-month holding pattern unless I gave up entirely.

"Bummer." Bitsy's dismissive tone made sense, considering. "Well, you'll figure something out. Meanwhile, you're a film star until Christmas." She hummed a little carol. "Just hear those sleigh-bells jingling." She looked up, that happy-face pasted in place. "Hey, you should see about getting a sleigh ride from that other hotel, Sleigh Bells Chalet. I heard …"

Bitsy cast a barrage of tourist ideas at me like they were a big draw to being in Wilder River—as if I had anyone with whom to share a parade of Christmas lights, a holiday time-capsule event, shopping in the snow, ice skating on a frozen river.

I signed the contract anyway.

Back at my apartment, I sprawled on my couch and reopened *Forfeit*, the Dick Francis novel about horse racing. To be honest, I knew nothing about horse racing, even though my dad had apparently been heavily involved in the losing side of it as part of his many indiscretions back in the day. The book stung a little for that reason, but the amateur sleuth hero—sports journalist Tyrone—had me hooked.

Before I could find out why the rival magazine's reporter jumped out the window, a text disrupted my reading.

It was from Danica.

I gave Grant Calhoun your number. I hope that's okay. He was asking Jeremy if he knew you.

My blood reversed direction in my veins. Normally, I would've been ticked, since I closely guarded my private number. But this was Danica. She had discretion—most of the time. With the clear exception of her blindness about Grant Calhoun.

Why? Did he say why he wanted it? I asked instead of railing on her like some part of me wanted to—or telling her I'd be there by Thursday to start work again, and to maybe beg Freya for another chance.

Grant Calhoun—who'd basically called me a cat lady and who'd more or less turned my next year to ashes—couldn't be asking for my number to ask me out.

Nope. You'll have to wait and see.

I gaped at Danica's string of texts, all my systems churning. What could it mean? I didn't have time to date, even Mr. Eleven-on-a-Ten-Scale. And besides—Grant Calhoun was Mr. Zero to me. Regardless of the fact I couldn't help my idiot-side being attracted to him.

Another text from Danica popped up.

But as a mild caution. Don't get your hopes up too high. He's notoriously uncatchable. Good thing you're fairly non-contagious yourself. She added a laugh-cry emoji.

I wasn't getting any hopes up—about his contacting me or about Grant himself. I wasn't going to try to catch Grant Calhoun. I'd sooner

43

trap a grizzly bear with a toothache than Grant Calhoun.

Worse, he didn't call or text me that night.

Chapter 6

Grant

Even though he was my oldest friend, Zed looked at me with one of those penny-pinching faces everyone from the top floor of the River Tresses Company wore when they broached the topic of expenditures.

"You've got to be kidding me," Zed said on the snowy Thursday afternoon in early October. "It's gone? All of it?"

"I've been doing a lot of experimenting."

Behind Zed, the huge plate-glass window of his corner office opened onto Mt. Wilder. I used to occupy this office and take in the view.

But the basement was good, too. It was where the company needed me most.

Zed would rather have had a hefty raise than the prestige of a corner office. He needed every penny for those medical bills for that kid of his.

"I thought the goal was to have a perfect shampoo for both shine and scalp health." For scalp health, I'd figured out the de-ionized water from the river, but we'd been testing the latest buzzword ingredients as well. Some came at hefty costs. Like the one I'd run us out of—and drawn Zed's scowl.

"Best hair health is a goal, sure. But how much of that Panukaa oil are you pouring in there? We can't exactly source that stuff and sell it under our brand. We're not a salon product. We're a drugstore brand."

"Yes, and we want to give the customers a salon-level product for a drugstore price, remember?" Unfortunately, Zed had caught me red-handed. I'd used up the lion's share of our Panukaa oil—and hadn't made significant progress.

"The question, Grant, is do *you* remember?" He rubbed the wrinkles in his forehead. "Okay, look. We can't have it shipped here, as you know."

"Company secret." I repeated the mantra. "So, should we plan another bro-trip to the southern hemisphere? Say, over Halloween? It'll be springtime there. Maybe we could take Dallin." Dallin was Zed's oldest son, the one whose medical condition racked up the bills. "He's a fan of those movies they filmed there."

Zed didn't even smile. "Don't you get it, Grant? There's no time for a bro-trip. We're working on a deadline. They want to roll this out by January one."

My veins popped and my head throbbed.

Roll it out! That meant—it meant the formula would have to be complete long before that. Or no later than December. I wasn't even close.

"Zed, you know as well as I do you can't put deadlines on science." Deadlines were for penny-pinchers and pencil-pushers, not people in the trenches who cared about safety and best outcomes. "A deadline on science doesn't make for good results. And we want *good results*."

"Deadlines on science put a man on the moon." Strong volley from Zed.

"That was a *political* deadline."

Zed lowered his voice and checked the empty hallway. "This is, too."

What? That didn't make sense. We were a hair-care product company, not a campaign for office. "What do you mean?"

"Word is, Gloss is launching a huge new product line. They claim to be adding a miracle ingredient that is going to blow up the hair care world. You have to beat them to it, Grant."

"Beat Gloss?" My mouth went dry. "GlossTastic commands the biggest market share in the whole country, both in salons and on drugstore shelves."

"Yes, beat Gloss." Zed's chin puckered beneath his grim frown. "Our biggest rival."

"Biggest rival? Are you delusional?" What a joke. "They're our *much bigger* rival. As in, if Sugarplum Falls Community College declared nationally ranked Alabama State University's Crimson Tide team as its rival. We're the peons the bigger team doesn't even know exist."

"I know, I know. I hear it all day long. River Tresses is the ant that Gloss squashes on the sidewalk without even looking down." His tone turned ominous. "Everything is at stake, Grant. Everything."

The blood in my veins changed directions.

When Zed said *everything*, he meant not only the latest product, but also the plant itself and the jobs tied to it.

Practically every job in this town either relied on tourism or the River Tresses plant. Tourism couldn't support everyone year-round.

"December first it is." New plant manager Bolton and the other people upstairs were dealing with pressure, and I was their guy, the one they depended on. Frankly, I'd been in their shoes. "So, what is Gloss's new miracle ingredient?"

Zed shook his head. "No details. Just rumors, and vague ones at that."

"Well, it'd better not be our liquid gold." We'd put all our eggs in the Panukaa oil basket. I'd tried everything with it, but nothing had quite gone right yet. *It needs something else.* The de-ionized water from Wilder River was a big find, though. A major step forward. "Zed, we have to get to New Zealand and source ourselves more of that Panukaa oil. Pronto."

"I'll book myself a flight." He zipped his lip. "And remember—mum's the word on Panukaa."

"What about me? Book my flight, too." During the multi-hour flight, I'd tell Zed about the awesome water discovery.

"You? You're never leaving the lab. Chain yourself to the stainless steel table leg, dude. I'll bring in a bedpan."

Gross. "But I'm the one you need to negotiate with the Panukaa orchard owner for the best price and greatest quantity we can get." That's how we'd done things last time. "Plus, time on the plane will let me think."

"Did time on the plane work for thinking things out in the past?"

No. It hadn't. I frowned at my admission of failure. "Well, giving me a deadline certainly won't help. You know me and mental blocks when under pressure."

Actually, Zed was the only one who knew. When it'd looked like I was about to choke in the final moments at the state championship football game, Zed had picked up on it. He'd distracted me by retelling me the plot of a sci-fi movie we both liked. He'd calmed me enough to put my mind at ease and win the game.

"You're going to have to tame those mental blocks yourself, man. Bolton and the others aren't springing for two tickets to New Zealand. Period."

Then how was I supposed to conquer this?

My inner voice, who I'd named Gandalf, spoke to me in crusty but wise tones. *Touching Roxanna Reid's hand last week did that for you, dude. You had a breakthrough right after that.*

Shush, Gandalf. I'd burned that bridge. I'd asked for her number from Danica, Jeremy's wife, intending to text her an apology, but I hadn't worked up the courage yet.

Cowardly way out, sure. But I hadn't slept well since the evening of the book club. I'd close my eyes at night, and the after-image always burned there was the trembling pout of her lip and the shocked hurt in her eyes. She deserved an apology.

"When more product gets here, I'll start experimenting again, then." My brain was that blocked for now.

"Bad idea." Zed shook his head. "I'll be back from New Zealand as fast as possible with more product, but if I'm leaving my wife to handle our Fearsome Five for ten days, you owe it to me personally to make huge progress."

My shoulders slumped. He wasn't wrong. And we wouldn't be in this situation if I hadn't been on a trip to Fantasyland thinking about pouty-lipped Roxanna Reid throwing snowballs to Dasher and used triple the required Panukaa oil the other day. The last bottle.

"Fine." I whooshed out a sigh. "I'll make major progress."

But how?

"Quit looking so forlorn. You've broken out of mental-block jail a million times in the past by just reading a book. Remember? Hello, your whole house is full of books. Go see your mom, grab some books, read a bit, and get unblocked. How long have we known each other? That's what has always worked in the past."

True. The lab was no place to break a mental block. I'd been laser focused on the formula.

Maybe I shouldn't have been.

But Zed had a point—the mini-brainstorm the other night had likely come from talking about Captain Vartigan, not from touching Roxanna Reid's fingertips and getting that electrifying synapse-connection. Coincidence. Pure coincidence.

"Maybe you're right. More distraction, less of the try-fail cycle."

"Dude, you know I'm right." Zed tapped his temple. "Other people aren't like you. They have to *focus* to get things done. You, on the other hand, need your conscious mind to be completely occupied so that your subconscious mind can work its magic."

"Then why did you tell me to chain myself to the lab table?"

"Just to watch your reaction." Zed guffawed in the donkey-laugh he'd perfected at age thirteen. He usually hid that specific talent, but he belted it at me. "It doesn't have to be reading. It can be movies, or

49

sports, or shoveling snow. Dating helped you a few times, so that's an idea. As long as it isn't Ivory."

"Don't worry. I posted a sign on the door of my soul: *No Ivorys allowed.*" Zed was right. About all of it. "Meanwhile, I'll line up all the distractions."

Zed left.

Gandalf whispered in his gruff, commanding voice. *The palm-touch electrification of Roxanna Reid might be the distraction you need. Consider her soft lips, but also those huge baby-deer brown eyes.*

Well, I would, except that there were the horrible cat sweaters to negate the pluses, but thanks anyway, Gandalf.

I'd stick to books.

But which books? I'd read all the Yardley Gregson books too many times. I needed something new and compelling. Something with twists and puzzles, and …

Uh-oh.

It hit me.

I headed over to the Hot Chocolate Shop.

"Just a second, Grant." Freya interrupted my texting. "Are you telling me you've changed your mind about joining Twelve Slays of Christmas?"

"Yes?" My voice cracked, like I was fourteen again. "I should've joined the other day when …"

"Yes, you should have."

"It was selfish."

"You did not have a Christmas spirit that slayed."

"That sounds weird, Freya." Freya should not use last year's teen slang. "Anyway, is the offer still open for Roxanna Reid if I join? I've read the book, and I'd be willing to bet she has too." She'd seemed so horrified about her unpreparedness—I would bet Roxanna had read not only tonight's Dick Francis book, but all the other books for the rest of the club's meetings. She just seemed the type. On the ball. Determined. Full of integrity.

"Sorry to disappoint you, Grant. I ran into Danica. She told me Roxanna Reid, *who didn't read*, isn't coming back to Wilder River anytime soon."

"Oh." I'd really blown it.

Freya said I could still join. The cuckoo clock chimed three times, so there were four hours left until tonight's meeting of the book club. I bought a couple of Hawaiian Ham Sliders and went to Mom's.

She liked it—against her will. "You haven't taken a bite of yours yet." She eyed mine, the greed making her lips smack. "If you're not going to eat it …"

I handed it over and went into Mom's kitchen, where I made a peanut butter and honey sandwich.

Roxanna smelled like honey. And I'd never see her again.

I had her number. If I used it, what would I say in my text? *I joined Twelve Slays of Christmas because I need you to touch my hand so I can get inspiration for a shampoo formula.*

Anything even less specific would be twice as lame.

I put my phone back in my pocket. The prospect of the book club didn't even brighten me.

Chapter 7

Roxanna

"That was perfect, Sanna." Domingo grinned. He had a strong, charming Barcelona accent, including the lisp. So he called me "Thanna" *insthead*. "You make it look easy, but I've worked with hundreds of models, and I know it's not. Well done."

The compliment washed over me too quickly. "If you want another segment, I can try again with a different expression."

Domingo held his camera at his chest. "Nope. We got it. We'll start at five tomorrow morning."

Which meant I needed to be in the styling chair by two thirty. "Great." I smiled. "You're a pleasure to work with."

He blushed. I rushed to my room, where I showered off the day and washed off the inch-deep layer of camera makeup. Then, tucked my hair up into its neat little hat. This time, I'd found one *without* a cat's face and ears, thank goodness. This time, it just had sparkly stars all over it. But it was, unfortunately, quite roomy, *á la* a poufy shower cap.

Basically, my hair had to be contained in a pouf-hat for two reasons. One, the NDA with Gordon Glass said so—since my hair made me recognizable everywhere as Sanna. Even in the remote wilds of Wilder River. And I was in enemy territory, or so Bitsy said. No one could know Gloss was shooting its commercials at the small but excellent Wilder River Ski Resort. That would be a big, wintry "unveiling" moment for the advertising department. I'd heard rumors it would launch on New Year's Eve right before the apple dropped in Times Square in New York City.

Gloss did things big.

Two—and more practically—my hair couldn't get tangled at the end of day one of filming. We had to shoot again tomorrow, and the hair team had only budgeted enough time to style, not to wash my hair. Whether other hair models washed their hair before every shoot, I had no idea. But Gloss had a policy of keeping as many natural oils in my hair as possible. *Adds to authenticity and shine,* they said.

Where was that Dick Francis novel? I'd read it—twice, but I needed another glance before going to Freya to beg for her mercy. If I needed to be in Wilder River until Christmas, it wouldn't hurt to ask to be in Twelve Slays of Christmas again. The worst she could say was no.

But when I tried seeing the text in the paperback, my eyes started watering. Must be dust in my contacts. I took them out and put on my ridiculously thick glasses. My eyes were already too large for my face—a detriment growing up that drew teasing, especially when my awful glasses made my eyes look like a character on a Japanese animated TV show.

Well, at this rate, Gordon Gloss had nothing to worry about. Even without Pouf Hat, I would look nothing like Sanna from the hair care billboards.

Downstairs, I met Danica, who'd offered to taxi me around when she had time.

"So?" she asked. "You're serious about my taking you to The Hot Chocolate Shop? After what happened last week with ...?"

"With Freya?" I filled in the blank before she could mention Grant. Who had *not* texted me. "Let's say I'm giving Freya one more chance to change her mind."

"What's your pitch going to be? Because I'm guessing it won't work."

"Thanks for the vote of confidence."

"You know I never give anyone false hope."

"Your honesty is a gift and a curse."

We turned the corner onto Main Street. It was lined with quaint buildings—a jewelry store, a bank, a newspaper office, that hotel Bitsy had mentioned, Sleigh Bells Chalet.

"Did Grant text you?"

Javelin to the heart.

"If you must know, Grant Calhoun is dead to me." Well, to every part of me except my endocrine response to his name and the memory of his touch and of his deep love for Yardley Gregson.

"Did you check your spam folder? Sometimes texts from unknown numbers get shunted off into Spamland."

To my everlasting shame, I had checked Spamland.

Daily.

Pathetic, but true.

Time to reclaim the subject. "Here's my pitch to Freya. This time around, I've read all of *Forfeit,* the assigned book for the week, *plus* three more horseracing novels by Dick Francis."

"Overachiever."

"Takes one to know one."

"That's why I love you. Why three more books?"

"Just so I can contribute better to the discussion, especially if there end up being diehard fans of the author in attendance."

"Diehard. At a crime novel book club. I get it, I get it."

Danica turned the final corner, and the Hot Chocolate Shop came into view. "Call me for a ride when it's over? Whenever that may be? I want to hear the outcome." She let me out in front of the dark-red, one-story building with the white trim, the lone pine tree, and the candles in the windows.

Smoke rose from the chimney.

Trudging toward destiny, I climbed the steps. Though there were only three, they stretched high. When I pushed open the door to the Hot

Chocolate Shop, the warm wall of cocoa-laced aroma slammed me, and Freya stood there.

I launched. "Freya? I read *Forfeit,* plus three more Dick Francis novels, and"—my eyes darted toward a shuffling sound near the fireplace, and landed on none other than—"Grant?"

Why was Grant Calhoun here? Blast that endocrine response that made my face flush and my upper lip perspire!

Grant's gaze pulled me toward him like a tractor beam until he bumped up against the edge of my space bubble. The beam tugged hard, urging me to step beyond the bubble's edge, but I locked my knee to halt myself.

Hey. This guy had rejected me publicly! He'd sunk my hopes of being in the book club. He'd strung me along. He'd asked for my number and then never used it.

In short, Grant Calhoun had me on the world's worst playground seesaw—and seeing him brought me down with a bump.

He was dead to me. Right?

Unfortunately, I was a hundred percent alive to his physical charms.

"Roxanna?" My name on his lips was like warm gingerbread with applesauce, sweet and spicy, hot and cold, filling and light all at once. "I thought you were never coming back to Wilder River."

He looked over at Freya, who wore one of those mysterious smiles where only the edges of the mouth curved upward.

My upper lip twitched. "My freelance job here was extended." I turned to Freya, but my eyes kept sticking to Grant's gorgeous face like they'd been velcroed there. "I'm here to ask for that second chance again."

Grant lifted his hand, palm outward, as if saying hello. The memory of when we'd touched palms flashed into my mind like a thousand spotlights. Was he remembering it too?

He pulled a sheepish smile. "Turns out, I'm here for a second chance, too. I decided to join Twelve Slays of Christmas." He darted a gaze toward Freya and then back to me. "But only if Freya lets you join, too."

Chapter 8

Grant

Where were Roxanna's cat clothes today? She looked almost normal. Well, except for the replacement hat. It was blessedly cat-ear-free, but it was weirdly poofy, like a mix between a towel turban and a chef's hat. Whatever, it was the baby-deer eyes that had me floating on air from the second she shocked me by setting foot in the shop. They were even larger than I remembered. Had she been wearing glasses before? Or had her pupils just dilated when she saw me?

Okay, and the pouting lip had me by the heartstrings, too.

Confound that pouting lip, I was its slave, if only for a split second. That plump, pink lip made me stare—and say something stupid: *I'm here for a second chance.* Luckily, I recovered and said that thing about joining the book club.

Okay, fine. So I'd sounded a little love-struck then, as well.

But I wasn't. I was there to get a solid distraction.

So far so good, pal, Gandalf snarked.

Oh, brother.

"Sit down, you two." Freya shooed us toward the wingback chairs. "That is, if you've both read the Dick Francis book for tonight's discussion."

"We have," I answered for both of us, since Roxanna mentioned she'd read *Forfeit,* plus the next two books in the series. Trying too hard? I'd say so under almost any other circumstances. But Freya was Freya, and Roxanna had insisted she needed to be in this group.

Why did she care so much? Shame on me, I hadn't even bothered to ask.

I could have at least tried to find out why she was desperate to join Twelve Slays—especially when she claimed to dislike crime fiction.

"You're both a half hour early." Freya brought us each a mug of her best hot chocolate with a look that asked, *Eager, much?* "Did the two of you pre-plan this?"

"No!" we both said at once.

"We're here to talk about the book." Roxanna held up her copy. "If you'll allow us both into the club."

Freya didn't tell us to leave, so I took that as a good sign. Instead, she said, "Save any of this week's book discussion until the other club members arrive."

"So"—Roxanna gulped visibly—"we're members?"

Freya closed her eyes briefly and gave a shallow nod.

We were in!

Roxanna Reid broke into a smile. And something happened— either to the fire in the hearth that shifted and popped, glowing suddenly brighter, or something happened to my insides. A shining light. Gandalf's chuckle sounded, and he quipped, *Go toward the light.*

Enough of that old tired joke.

I sipped the hot chocolate. The theobromine hit my bloodstream extremely fast.

Or, was that Roxanna's nearness? She was a full foot away, and I swear, when the space heater angled just right, her honey scent enveloped me.

"Theobromine is the principal alkaloid of the cacao bean," I said in a geeky non sequitur.

"And it's the principal alkaloid of the love brew that the Chylockian King uses to attempt to woo the Rygraff Princess—and

58

nearly succeeds, until Captain Vartigan rescues her by fighting off the Beast."

Good grief, I was captured! Frankly, I was practically pinging off the walls. "Uh-huh," I pressed the rim of the mug to my lips, staring at hers.

Roxanna leaned in close and whispered, "There has to be more to Freya's delicious hot chocolate, though. I wonder what her secret ingredient is. It's key, I'm sure."

Secret key ingredients popped me back to my laboratory problem. But, no. I couldn't focus on that. I had to live in the moment here, as we launched into a conversation about books adapted to movies—and whether they were a success or a failure for us as readers first.

Focus on the moment. Easy, considering what a highly sensory moment Roxanna was giving me. The smells of both honey and the wood fire. The sight of Roxanna's well-of-wisdom-and-hope eyes. The taste of this intoxicating chocolate brew. The touch of Roxanna's knee against mine when she shifted positions. The sound of her intelligent voice.

For the first time in weeks, it seemed like the locked door in my brain had unlocked. It hadn't *opened* yet, but it could.

Freya brought over a plate of goodies that Roxanna had ordered. There was a chocolate croissant, a hot Hawaiian ham and Swiss slider, and a cream cheese danish with raspberries.

"Wow, I didn't realize how large these three would be when I ordered. Would you like one? Or two?"

Honestly, the woman could use the calories from all three. She was just this side of too thin.

"Thanks." I took half of one. "This is good." The croissant was buttery and flaky, with a dark chocolate filling as rich as the hot chocolate in the mug. "I keep getting the Hawaiian Ham Sliders instead, but thanks for helping me branch out."

Freya returned from topping off our mugs from one of the kettles. "Twelve Slays of Christmas has six members, including me, and now the two of you." She named Quentin, the owner of Quality Jewelers on Main Street, Bing and his wife Ellery Whitmore of the Sleigh Bells Chalet, and a woman who worked at the ski lodge. I didn't know any of them personally. "Oh, and a surgeon working at the hospital. Cody Haught."

Roxanna perked up. "Really? Cody Haught? I went to college with him back as an undergraduate. Everyone knew him." Her cheeks pinked.

Somewhere behind my ribcage, a lion roared to life. I hated the guy already, if he could create that response in Roxanna.

"Never met him." I took a big chomp of the croissant to keep myself from saying anything incriminating.

While chewing, I mulled over my weird reaction. I hardly knew the woman. Basically, I'd been rude to her a week ago, and now, I guess I felt like I had to spend the rest of … however long making it up to her.

That, or I might be genuinely interested in her. After all, she did have an encyclopedic knowledge of Yardley Gregson's stories. What wasn't there to enchant a fantasy-reading geek like me about that? And touching her hand had made me feel like I could solve any problem in the world.

Roxanna Reid certainly didn't fit the mold of any woman I'd dated. In other words, *the type of woman I refuse to look at anymore.*

For one, she didn't seem to be coming on to me. Most women flirted with me. Instead, she'd blushed at the mention of a different man, not me. Cue my internal caveman growl.

For another, she didn't dress like she was about to head out clubbing every day of the week. Cat sweaters, anyone? Not my usual female interest's wardrobe.

For another, she didn't overdo the makeup or flaunt thousand-dollar salon work on her hair. In fact, I hadn't even *seen* her hair, other than the one lock that escaped now and then that she swiftly tucked back inside the chef's hat she wore tonight. It could be a thatch-patch.

Instead of being image-conscious, she just seemed comfortable being her fantasy-novel-reading self.

To be honest, that *self* had me spinning, at least when it came to the mention of a rival. If Cody Haught even *was* a rival. More caveman growls.

We talked comfortably—or uncomfortably, in my case—for the next few minutes, and much as I didn't want to admit it, her words and thoughts and the whole Roxanna package grew increasingly appealing. Especially her thoughts.

"This shop feels like perpetual Christmas to me." She sipped at the edge of her mug. "The opposite of Narnia."

"Where it was always winter and never Christmas?" I asked, confirming the literary reference. "C.S. Lewis was great at creating a longing for Christmas."

Once again, we bonded over more fantasy authors we'd read.

"Why this book club, Roxanna? You seemed desperate to join, but didn't you tell me you don't like crime fiction?"

Her cup froze halfway to her lips. "The story question of mystery novels is almost always *will justice prevail.*" Her words were tight, clipped.

She hadn't exactly answered the question. "And?"

"And ... that story question, or real-life question, is always a little tough for me."

I took another bite of croissant, the last bite, and again waited for her to expound. The partial answer more or less shocked me, considering that Roxanna's cat-lady attire from last week would have put her in the perfect disguise as an avid reader of *The Cat Who* mysteries by Lillian Jackson Braun, which my mom used to read before she got addicted to game shows when her eyesight got bad.

She didn't expound. Instead, she gazed into the fire and started a new topic.

"It's funny. The only time my dad ever built a fire in our fireplace at home was Christmas Eve, so that might be why it feels Christmassy here." Her voice had a sad tinge to it, even though she followed with, "That's a sweet memory. I think we need more blazing hearths in modern life." She went on, describing the benefits of radiation from fires, how the yellow and red lights create natural endorphins, and how these days everyone is being subjected to blue light from screens instead.

"No wonder they call it campfire therapy." I sipped my hot chocolate. She still hadn't explained her conflicted feelings about justice. Maybe someday.

"Campfire therapy." The flames' reflections caught in her eyes, flickering, and the deep-brown irises shone with gold.

She sighed and smiled slightly. It lit something in me again. "Luckily, in Wilder River, we still light a lot of fires." My belly went warm, as if I'd subconsciously intended a double meaning about lighting fires.

"I'll bet you do." A little mirth danced at the edge of her smile.

The door jingled. Quentin, the owner of Quality Jewelers, and the couple from Sleigh Bells Chalet, Bing and Ellery Whitmore, came in.

My moment with Roxanna ended.

Pity. Just when I was feeling a connection.

"Whodunnit, folks? Who?" Quentin reminded me of Colonel Sanders with his white hair and big smile. "Don't spoil it until we start our discussion." He settled onto an armchair and immediately put his feet on the ottoman.

"Who has the kids?" Freya brought Bing and Ellery mugs of hot chocolate. They held hands and said this was their date night—and they'd hired a sitter for both the hotel and their baby daughters.

"Sleigh Bells Chalet?" Roxanna asked. "Do you actually offer sleigh rides?"

"We do. Our stables manager Lenny is also boss of the sleigh. Call me and I'll set you up with a ride sometime," Ellery said. "Bing has a beautiful team, Donner and Blitzen."

"I'd *love* that." Roxanna practically sparkled when she said so.

The sparkle is nice, Gandalf pointed out. *You could make her sparkle, you know.*

Oh, brother.

"Okay, time to start." Freya came over and handed out the discussion questions, and the book club was underway, with only the five of us. Fly-in-the-ointment Cody Haught hadn't showed up. "We have to start without Dr. Haught, as he's still in surgery."

He was a surgeon?

I can't compete with a surgeon.

Hey, I wasn't competing! This was a book club, not a competition. Besides, I had a formula to produce, not a heart to fight for.

Freya lifted her list of pre-printed questions. "Let's begin with character reaction. Did you love or hate Tyrone, and why?"

"He's complex," Roxanna answered. "He cares for his invalid wife like a true hero, but he cheats on her the first chance he gets?"

No wonder we had to all read the book before attending. The debate heated up about Tyrone—with Quentin on the *I hate him* side, as a widower, and with Freya playing devil's advocate.

Next, we talked about setting. The Whitmores had a lot to say about the horse business, considering they owned Whitmore Stables and had lived in the horse breeding and racing worlds.

Just as I was about to offer my not-so-expert opinion on the drugging Tyrone underwent during a key plot point, the door jingled. A confident man breezed through the door, with cocky surgeon written all over him.

"Sorry I'm late." He swaggered over to the armchair next to Roxanna's side of the loveseat and plunked down. "What did I miss? Oh, hi, Roxanna. What's up with the hat?"

She turned beet red, I swear. Redder than Santa Claus's suit. That, or I just saw red since he'd blazed out with the question that had been burning the tip of my tongue but I'd been too chicken to ask. Man, I needed to get a handle on this overreaction. Anesthetize the possessive rage—and fast.

"Nothing," Roxanna said, patting at her head and around the edges of the brim or whatever. She poked a stray brown lock back inside. "You missed the first ten minutes of book discussion." She turned away from Dr. Cody Haught, pointedly ignoring him.

Good for her. Meanwhile, my insecurity shifted into high gear.

He's a doctor, for crying out loud. All women want doctors, right? I'm nothing but a lab worker these days, no managerial title listed along with my name anymore. He's a surgeon with incredible swagger. I'm a nerd who can only talk about sci-fi books and insult her. Oh, and destroy her dreams.

Compared to Cody Haught, I didn't stand a chance. And if she gave Cody the instant cold shoulder, what could I expect?

I folded my arms over my chest, missing the next three minutes of discussion, until Ellery Whitmore asked me a direct question. "Do you think Tyrone's wife made the right choice at the end of the book?"

Tyrone? Who was Tyrone? It took me a bit to reconnect with where I was—and not on Planet Jealousy. "I wouldn't have done it." He'd cheated on his invalid wife, and she'd forgiven him.

The clock struck eight and our discussion ended.

"Take these for next week." Freya handed us all copies of the book *Unpleasantness at the Bellona Club* by Dorothy Sayers. "Lord Peter Wimsey is quite different from Tyrone. Read up."

Quentin, Bing and Ellery, and Cody Haught—blessedly—left. Good riddance.

Just when I expected Roxanna to head out after them, she didn't.

The two of us remained, sitting in front of the fire. Like a dingbat trying to mimic my rival, I asked a burning but lame question. "Do you have a cat?"

Roxanna looked up from her open copy of next week's novel. "A what? No."

"Whew."

"What do you mean, *whew?*"

Not that I should be so relieved about her not having a cat. That was ridiculous. It wasn't that I didn't like cats. Well, maybe a little dislike, but I did like dogs more. "What about a dog?"

"I'm not home often enough to take care of pets."

Huh, what kind of job did she have that kept her traveling and out so much she couldn't even have a pet? "Freelance work?"

She nodded. "But about dogs, I always wanted a dog when I was a kid," she said, "and I finally got one when I was about to graduate from high school. A registered Samoyed. Yeti. Great dog. I love Yeti. He has the best smile. And his tail curls!" She let out a sigh of love, penetrating me. Cutting me to the quick.

All signs point to the fact I'm absolutely interested in her.

"But—you said you don't have a dog."

"Yeah, I know. To be brief, there was some chaos."

"Chaos?"

"Life stuff, you know. Basically, I had to sell a few things— including Yeti."

A heat sloshed through my stomach, followed by a hint of nausea. What did *there was some chaos* mean, exactly? What was *life stuff?* Obviously, she'd been through something really hard if she'd had to sell a beloved dog.

"I have a Golden Retriever, not a Samoyed, and not registered, but he's out in the back of my truck. Would you"—the words got stuck in my craw until I gulped twice—"like to meet him?"

Her eyes lit up. "Really?" She jumped to her feet, and we went out to my old truck.

Wow, my truck really was old. *What kind of car does Cody Haught drive? A Porsche probably. Surgeons drive Porsches.*

"Oh, look at you! Good boy!" Instead of waiting for me to keep up, Roxanna rushed to the tailgate, climbed right up on the bumper, stepped over and loved on Dasher like he was her long-lost best friend.

Dasher took to her instantly, letting her rub his neck and belly, soaking up all her attention.

"What's your name, boy? You're so beautiful. Look at your shiny

65

coat. Somebody takes good care of you." The patter went on, and—idiot me—I soaked up all the compliments meant for Dasher.

"Dasher likes you."

"I *love* him." She buried her face in his neck. "Don't I, Dasher?" To which he barked once. "We should play catch sometime, Dasher. I'll throw the ball and you can bring it back to me."

I froze. Her suggestion mirrored my little fantasy about snowball-catch with Dasher, the one I'd envisioned the first day I met Roxanna.

My face blazed like it was being hit with Captain Vartigan's heat ray.

The town hall clock struck ten. The shop's porch light snapped off, and Freya came out the front door, locking it behind her. "You two are still here, huh? Hi, Dasher."

Dasher barked back.

"This is a sweet dog." Roxanna gave him one last scrub behind his ears. "But it's late. I should go." She whipped out her phone and dialed. Danica's voice answered. "Finished finally. See you soon." Roxanna slid it back into her pocket. "Danica's on her way. You can head out. Right, Dasher? You want to go home?"

She was only talking to the dog, while I chewed on the bitter taste of a missed chance. I should have offered to take Roxanna home. Or to wherever she was staying during her freelance job here.

Next time. For sure, I'd offer to take her home next time. No missed opportunities.

Danica pulled up within moments, her wipers clearing newly falling snow from her van's windshield. When had it started snowing? I'd been so caught up in Roxanna.

"Can I help you down from the truck?" I asked. When I reached up to take her hand, our palms met again. That familiar energy surged—maybe not as electrocuting as before, but still enlightening.

The inner Gandalf voice repeated itself. *The formula is lacking a key ingredient.*

"See you next week?" I asked Roxanna.

"I can't miss it."

What did that mean?

Roxanna rode away in Danica's van. I watched for a bit until the taillights disappeared.

All sorts of key ingredients floated through my brain. Gandalf chortled, *Roxanna Reid might be one of them.*

Chapter 9

Roxanna

It wasn't that the Dorothy Sayers novel *Unpleasantness at the Bellona Club* was dull. It wasn't. Lord Peter Wimsey was a fantastic hero, but that darn mattress at the Wilder River Lodge was just so … sinkable. It sank me into instant deep rest. I couldn't read there—ever.

I had to be able to make good points during our discussion, and with only one read-through, I hadn't pinpointed my feelings about the text yet.

There had to be another reading location option, or I'd sleep again, *and* I'd be kicked out of Freya's club—again. I got the impression simply *reading* the novel wasn't sufficient. Freya put people on the spot.

"Library, please?" I climbed into the taxi parked in the circle in front of the lodge Thursday late afternoon, as soon as shooting wrapped for the latest Gloss commercial, the one where wardrobe had me in a white faux-fur coat, thank goodness. It was the first time I'd been warm at work in ages.

"You look familiar. Are you local?" The driver looked at me in the rear-view mirror. "Super familiar."

"Nope." I shoved my thick glasses higher on my nose. "In town for business." Argh, I shouldn't have even said that much, according to the

NDA. "But people tell me that a lot. I must have one of those faces God reused."

The driver wasn't deterred. "I never forget a face." He tapped his chin as we stopped at a four-way stop sign. Thank goodness Wilder River was billboard-free, or he would've likely seen me.

Fortunately, it didn't dawn on him soon enough, and we arrived at the Wilder River Public Library first.

"Thanks for the ride, even though I'm a nobody." I tipped him extra, praying he got the hint to stop trying to figure out who I was.

With my paperback copy of the Dorothy Sayers novel in hand, I found a quiet nook with a stiff chair and a hard laminate-topped table—the polar opposite seating of my suite at the lodge. There, I flew through the next six chapters to the midpoint. There, the story turned, and something about it lambasted me with a memory of Dad's experience, crippling my reading speed.

Nothing in the story exactly mirrored events in my real past filled with betrayal and courtrooms and destroyed trust—but for whatever reason, this time I got all choked up.

"No," I wheeze-whispered. I snapped the book shut and shoved it to the center of the table. A torrent of tears threatened, and I sniffed twice as if that could hold them back.

"Hey, are you all right?" Grant loomed over me.

I blinked back tears, pasted on a grin. "Grant Calhoun? At the library?"

"You look upset." He pulled out a chair and sat down beside me. "You're reading Peter Wimsey, not the sixth book in the Vartigan Chronicles where the Rygraff Queen thinks Vartigan is dead and offers to sacrifice herself to the pagan gods to bring him back to life."

I sniffled, and a little laugh bubbled up in return. "That is one sad book."

"Bad cliffhanger, too. Can you believe he made us wait a full six months for the sequel?"

"Cruel and unusual." I brushed my cheeks nonchalantly. They

were dry, thank goodness. "Are you finished with the novel for tonight's meeting?" Just hearing about Yardley Gregson's stories made my tears recede.

Grant wrinkled his nose. It made him look fifteen—and so cute. "That's why I'm here. At work, I kept getting phone calls and emails."

"Where do you work?"

"I'm a chemist." He didn't say where. "Is it cheating if we rent a viewing room and borrow the movie of *Unpleasantness at the Bellona Club* and watch it?"

There was a movie? "It's definitely cheating," I said.

And yet, ten minutes later, we were seated in a darkened room on a small couch with the BBC logo looming and the credits naming stars of the movie version of our assigned book. "Thanks for cheating with me."

Um, that hadn't come out quite right. In fact, I didn't even know whether Grant had someone else in his life.

"Are you married?" he asked, as if triggered into the same train of thought by my lame comment. "I'm single."

The actor portraying Lord Peter appeared on screen, debonair and Art Deco to the hilt, and slightly reminiscent of Grant with the noble air and the breadth of shoulders.

"I'm single, too." I inhaled a little too deeply, and Grant's scent wafted through all my thoughts. Clean and pepperminty, like a candy cane with a side of spice gumdrops. *Grant Calhoun is candy.*

Our shoulders pushed a little uncomfortably against each other's. I leaned slightly forward, and he took my cue—slipping his arm across the back of the sofa. For a full minute of screen time, I stayed angled forward, but then gravity overtook me, and I found myself sinking backward against his arm. It flexed, pulling me to him, and guess who wasn't paying any attention to the Bellona Club?

My mouth went as dry as Lord Peter's martini.

A few minutes later, his head fell against my shoulder. His breathing grew regular and—eep! He'd fallen asleep?

The temptation to rest my cheek against him surged, and I resisted for about thirty seconds of screen time before sinking against him, picturing his touch, his kiss, his …

No! I pulled my head back.

I couldn't let that happen. Not any of it. I couldn't be close physically with someone I couldn't be fully honest with. Please! Under the current circumstances, I couldn't even tell him what my job was.

Deception was *not* my thing in relationships—family or romantic or professional. Period. I'd endured enough deception from others to make sure I'd never be the one to commit it.

Sure, the physical attraction was undeniable, but if, like Danica claimed, he was everybody's type, then I was just being sucked into his charisma vortex, right?

I willed my head to remain upright, pulling against his gravity, resisting valiantly. That was, until—

Grant Calhoun snuggled against me with a masculine groan.

It undid my defenses, and my cheek dropped sideways again, falling against his soft, wavy hair. Mmm, the mint and gumdrops filled my senses again, and I rested my eyes, picturing Grant waking up, taking me in his arms, and giving me a kiss that expanded my soul.

I must have made some kind of satisfied sound because Grant inhaled sharply.

"Did I miss something?" He sat up.

Luckily, he'd been fast asleep. Had he even noticed my momentary lapse into the luxury of his embrace?

"Sorry," he said. "I was already past this point in the book, so I must have dozed."

"Be honest, did you read it?" I paused the show.

"Of course I read it. Freya is great, but she's scary." He blinked a few times, and then he looked down to where his arms were still circled around me. "Oh." He scratched his neck, looking like he was acting as though he planned to pretend that embrace hadn't occurred. "Did you read it?"

"Are you kidding? I came down to the library to read through it

71

again, just for safety's sake. If I get kicked out of Twelve Slays of Christmas, my whole education is basically chestnuts roasted to cinders on an open fire."

"What does that even mean?"

I confessed to him about the edict handed down from Dr. Higgins.

"Higgins?" He gave a sniff. "Even I've heard of the legendary Henrietta Higgins, and I didn't go to college there." He mentioned a Higgins legend that had traveled beyond campus. Something about the professor who required everyone in a class to read *Anna Karenina, War and Peace,* and *Crime and Punishment* in a single weekend.

Sounded about right. "She does love Russian lit—and awful translations of it, at that." I told him about the Walpole Translation.

"Seriously? That's just crimes against literature. Anyway, you can't change cooperating professors?"

"I wish." I told him about the roadblocks to my Plan B—my becoming a college literature professor—without actually telling him about my current career. "I'll get there. When I do, I know my mom will be smiling down on me."

"She's gone?" he asked.

"I never knew her. She died after giving birth to me." I only knew what people told me about her. People like Grandma. Things like Mom's dream was to teach college English literature classes. "My dad raised me." Until his incarceration, but I didn't mention that humiliating fact.

"My dad got sick and passed away when I was little. They'd had me really late in life. My mom raised me."

"What's she like?"

His voice brightened. "My mom? Anyone who meets her never forgets her. She's an equal mixture of inspiring and wacky. I love her. I'll never *understand* her, but I love her."

Huh. A guy who loved his mom and freely admitted it. Whoa.

"Do any of us understand our parents?" I asked, knowing full-well I'd never comprehend my dad or his motives or what made him tick.

And commit corporate espionage egregious enough to spend years behind bars.

"No, but if I'm right, we all feel the weight of our forebears' expectations."

True enough. "And a few other weights." When he gave me an inquisitive look, I debated. Tell Grant Calhoun about Dad? Um, no. But I would say this much, "Sometimes I wish parents would worry half as much about disappointing their children as we do about disappointing them."

He rubbed his clean-shaven chin. "Don't you think they do?"

Obviously not, at least in my dad's case. "Hard to say."

"Do you see that painting?" He pointed through the tinted window to a portrait that hung in the main room. "The one of the stern-faced pioneer man?"

Sure, I saw it. "Who is it? Famous person?" Had to be, or he wouldn't be hanging in the public library, right?

"That's Richard Grant Wilder. I'm his second-great-grandson."

"And his namesake?" When Grant nodded, I asked, "Why is he hanging in the library?" Another sentence that could easily be misconstrued. "Why is his *picture* hanging in the library?"

Grant's features sobered. "He founded Wilder River."

"Impressive. And?" I asked, since there was obviously more to it. "You admire him for it?"

"It's one of those things you were saying a second ago—*weight of expectations.*"

"Did you ever even meet him? Does he expect something from you?" Grant couldn't have met him. The cragged pioneer face had to have passed out of this world long before Grant's time. "Or is this something you've taken on yourself?"

"Does it make any difference?"

Maybe not. "What are you trying to do for him?"

He tilted his head to the side. "It has to do with work stuff." He looked down at his lap, which held his upside-down copy of *The*

Bellona Club.

I wished he'd trust me with more about his family's expectations.

To be perfectly honest, Grant Calhoun fascinated me.

He wasn't just a good-looking guy. He wasn't just the resume that Danica had rattled off to me about his athleticism and his work ethic. He seemed driven by something far more deeply rooted, as if it came from his eternal identity.

The fact he had no idea that I was a model and therefore placed no expectations on me about celebrity didn't hurt my fascination level, either. I could just be myself, Roxanna Reid, with him.

Grant might be creeping beyond Eleven on that proverbial Ten Scale—to a Twelve. Or even a Thirteen. *If I get his number, I'll code-name him Mr. T in my phone.*

"It's all right, Grant. I can respect your priv—"

The door of the room swung open.

"Excuse me? Is this room—" A woman wearing stage makeup burst through the door. Her platinum hair flowed over her ample and overly exposed décolletage, and she sported the shortest miniskirt this side of a tennis match. None of it appropriate for winter weather in Wilder River. "As I live and breathe. Grant Calhoun. Is that you?"

"Ivory," he said, as though his trachea were collapsing.

Ivory!

My inner lioness roared to life. Ivory Keyes? And she knew Grant?

Chapter 10

Grant

I was drowning. Lung-choking memories of dating Ivory flooded back in a sludgy tidal wave full of rotting debris.

What was Ivory doing in a *library*?

Nevertheless, rote courtesy training took over and I stood, just like mom had taught me, when Ivory entered the room. Though Ivory was no lady.

"Hey, Ivory." I managed a nonchalant tone. Probably. Minus the voice-crack, sure. "Long time no see." *Wish it had been longer.*

Ivory's finger traced her exposed collarbone. "It's practically Christmas already. A full year since we broke up."

Ahem. Since *she* broke up with me—the very day I told her I'd taken the job at the laboratory and quit the management position at River Tresses—she could've clarified. The day she rage-wrote that holiday song she released on her social media feeds, which propelled her to online fame, feeding her already monstrous ego.

"Who's that?" She spared Roxanna a glance, lifting her chin and nose.

"This is Roxanna," I said, but Roxanna remained partially behind me.

"Oh." Ivory pulled a split-second smile. "Hi, Rowena." She angled so Roxanna was excluded from our conversation—a conversation my fight-or-flight instincts longed to flee.

"So, Grant. I saw your name on the room reservation. I've been looking all over town for you. Your truck is parked out front, so I came in."

Stalkeresque. Not her usual style. What did she want? My guts roiled. My brain shouted, *I'm still the nerd you recoiled from, not the town's rich businessman athlete you assumed me to be.*

Instead, I dug deep and located a shallow reservoir of good manners. "How have you been?"

"Let's talk. Please, Grant?" Her lower lip protruded, a trick which triggered a confused response somewhere at the back of my chest— flutters combined with pinching. In place of butterflies, wasps. "Can we go outside? They're closing any minute. That harpy Amaretta at the front desk announced it twice. She also told me I was in dress code violation. Doesn't she know this is a Rudolph original?"

Closing. Was it already seven? Book club!

"I have plans, Ivory." I picked up my coat and handed Roxanna hers. We closed up the room and walked toward the exit, with Ivory— unfortunately—gluing herself to my side and not getting the message my body language shouted: *buzz off.*

"I mean, Rudolph! Seriously!" she huffed, as though she'd been wronged. I had no choice but to hear her complaint. If the library was closing, Roxanna and I had to leave, too. "It's so obviously his design. He'd be totally insulted."

"I doubt that." Roxanna spoke so softly that Ivory might not have even heard. "He's way too humble to take offense."

We'd come to the glass doors of the exit into the night air, and Ivory stopped cold.

"What did you say?" Ivory's narrowed eyes burned a hole into Roxanna. "What do *you* know about Rudolph? Look at your hat."

Well, honestly, I couldn't fault Ivory's assessment of the hat. It wasn't a chef's hat this week, or even a Cat Hat special. This time? Roxanna wore one of those hunter's hats with the flaps on each side,

76

like Elmer Fudd's.

However, to my surprise, Roxanna didn't shrink from the insult. Instead, she gave Ivory one piercing glance and raised an eyebrow. Then, Roxanna headed out onto the dark sidewalk toward my truck.

The brush-off didn't shock me so much as Ivory's response to it. Ivory froze, as if her stiletto heels had bored holes into the threshold of the library's exit. "What?" she whispered, as if choked by gall.

The sliding doors closed and smacked her before sliding back open.

"Ouch," she whispered. She took a step forward, but only enough to be out of sliding-door danger. "That's not Rowena."

Twenty paces on, Roxanna slowly turned toward us from her position near my truck's passenger door. I hadn't offered her a ride to the book club, but it seemed like she expected one.

Fine with me.

Ivory stalked over to her, eyes narrow and suspicious. "What did you say about Rudolph?"

Roxanna brushed her hand beneath her chin. "Rudolph keeps his ego in check. He's more about the people his clothing serves than about having his fans serve him. That's part of why he's so successful."

"I guess you spend a lot of time reading his P.R." Ivory's tone reeked with toxicity. "Good for you."

Just then, Roxanna stepped forward into the glow of the library's exterior light, and a halo lit her face. The baby-deer eyes caught the gleam, and they reflected back that golden warmth. I sucked in a breath. The wasps all morphed back into butterflies in my chest, softening and floating. Wow, in this light, even Roxanna's bad hat didn't matter. There was a wisdom and kindness in her eyes that captivated me.

"Oh!" Ivory gasped beside me. "I'm so sorry." She backed up two steps, her heel catching between two sections of sidewalk cement and nearly toppling.

Instead of cursing or getting haughty and flipping her silken blonde hair over her shoulder like I'd seen her do a thousand times when confronted by a rival, Ivory gulped visibly, and she blinked her too-thick black fringe of eyelashes. "Nice to meet you, Roxanna."

What in the world? In half an instant, Ivory had morphed from queen bee into a humble suppliant at Roxanna's royal court. She'd even called Roxanna by her real name, instead of Rowena. Ivory always referred to other women by close-match wrong names, a habit I hadn't noticed until we'd been dating a full month, and which should've raised more red flags a lot sooner. Flags the size of Santa's world-wide toy sack.

Why would Ivory kowtow to Roxanna all of a sudden? My Spidey senses tingled.

Roxanna came over and threaded her arm through the crook of my elbow. "Grant and I are going to the Hot Chocolate Shop to discuss books. Would you like to join us? Have you ever read Dorothy Sayers?"

My arm flexed involuntarily. The honeyed scent of Roxanna wafted to me, and my shoulders straightened. Was Roxanna pretending to belong to me?

Should this bother me? It didn't. At all.

In fact, I felt stronger. More masculine and capable—even though her move to my side had obviously been a protective one.

"No, that's okay." Ivory affected her signature puppy-dog sympathy-solicitation look. "I read lots of other things. Fashion and celebrity articles. Comments on my posts. Not books."

Roxanna pasted on a beatific smile. "You're missing out. Books are one of life's biggest joys." She pulled herself flush against me. A breeze gifted me the scent of her skin. *Honeysuckle*. And intoxicating.

That scent turned off my brain, made me forget that Ivory, of all people, stood gaping at us. All I could think was *honey, honey, honey.*

Roxanna gave me a gentle tug, and we sidestepped Ivory, who muttered a weak goodbye.

I opened the passenger side door of my truck for Roxanna, then climbed in and started the engine. Ivory remained under the streetlight, as if transfixed, as we drove toward the Hot Chocolate Shop.

Finally, I could talk again.

"What are you, the Ivory Whisperer?" And where had Roxanna been while Ivory was ruining my life with her false expectations of who I was or should be? And singing them in that angry tone to the holiday tune?

"Whatever Ivory Keyes did to you, it's in the past."

"Wow. Was I that transparent?" My head had known for over a year that Ivory wasn't for me, but until three minutes ago, my heart hadn't been fully convinced. "Thanks for what you did back there."

"Of course. But you really shouldn't date witches like that."

"How do you know she's a witch?"

"Ivory? She runs a massive social media feed."

I'd heard as much, though I'd never looked at it myself, since she'd launched it the day of our breakup, catapulting to instant fame. Looking it over would've just been poisonous for me.

"Does having a big following on social media make her a witch?" Lots of things made her a witch in person, but wouldn't she hide those qualities when she was online and trying to present a highlight reel?

"No, but the fact that she uses it to bash people she dislikes makes her one. Celebrities and models are frequent targets. They have feelings too, you know."

"You follow her?"

"No, but a few people have sent clips of her to me, and I wish they hadn't." She looked at me harder. "She not only talks about famous people, she mentions locals." By the pointed look Roxanna leveled at me, it became clear Ivory's song had reached Roxanna. It must have been one of the clips. A sick heat sloshed in my belly. "She's not worthy of you, Grant."

"Oh." I couldn't formulate a more articulate response because my brain was shouting too loudly.

Roxanna thinks I'm worthy.

My knee quivered, which made the truck lurch. I steeled it, then steered the truck toward the Hot Chocolate Shop. When we parked, I took my time walking around to her side, catching my breath, ordering my emotions. Was I usually an emotional person? Nope. But being around Roxanna Reid chipped away at the block of stone of my soul and revealed new facets of the sculpture inside—the sculpture that might be the real me.

We went inside, and we discussed Dorothy Sayers. But all I could focus on was sitting close to Roxanna, inhaling Roxanna, drinking in the sight of her lower lip's plump pout. Every comment she offered dripped with brilliance. Everything about her seemed covered in delicate gold leaf.

I was falling for her. Hard.

While Quentin remarked on Lord Peter Wimsey's involvement in solving the mystery of the death at the Bellona Club, all I could do was revel in the warmth soaking into me from where Roxanna's thigh was pressed against mine. Was it just me, or was Roxanna sitting even closer to me than usual on the loveseat in front of the fire? I slipped my arm across the back of the little sofa, but I didn't let it slip against her shoulders.

I didn't let my arm wrap around her waist.

It cried out to wrap around her waist.

I forced it to stay in place.

The meeting ended, and Freya handed out copies of Sir Arthur Conan Doyle, which was the next week's book selection. Everyone else left. Roxanna stood to go.

"Can I drive you home?" I asked.

"That would be great." She smiled, and the whole room caught on fire. Or maybe that was just me. "I'm staying at the Wilder River Lodge tonight." She looked nervous all of a sudden, like she probably shouldn't have told me where she was staying.

"The lodge is really nice. Do you like it?"

"So far, yes. It's expensive, so I will probably have to look for a bed-and-breakfast or something for my next freelance visit."

"There's a next time?" My pulse surged.

"Yes, so I should be here several days next week."

"Do you have any nights free?" I'd been working late for weeks, but being with Roxanna was the ultimate distraction. I hadn't panicked about the formula all day. "If it's okay, I'd like to spend time with you."

She lowered her lashes, and when she lifted her eyes to meet mine, I was gifted her smile again. "Sure. That would be absolutely great."

Yes! We left the Hot Chocolate Shop, carrying our copies of the Sherlock Holmes assignment. I lingered a step behind, gazing at her hand, that same aching to touch her, to take it in mine.

Why this sudden rush of need for contact?

Gandalf chuckled. *She said you were worth more than a person like Ivory deserved. That's why.*

Truth clanged like a gong. Roxanna Reid cared about me. And, with the talk in the library—about being beholden to expectations, about caring about the family legacies we'd been given—I was starting to care about her, too.

More than I would've expected.

And that smile of hers. It slayed me more than the Twelve Slays of Christmas. I lay at her feet. It was like I'd seen it a million times before in my dreams.

I get to see her again. Soon! Was it a date? Was it *many* dates?

Chapter 11

Roxanna

Monday evening, I collapsed after a full day of shooting a commercial with Domingo, after an early morning of styling and then stretching way past sundown and into twilight.

"I like that enigmatic smile of yours," Domingo said with his Barcelona lisp. "You're the Mona Lisa of the snowy mountainside today. You see someone you love in your mind's eye. You have a secret."

Mind's eye was right. I hadn't seen Grant Calhoun in five days, if I counted the part of last Thursday after he'd dropped me off. Every partial day without him counted as *not with Grant*.

It was nuts.

But, for whatever reason, my soul stretched out to him. We'd bonded in the library. We'd been so simpatico in our views about life and responsibility and family honor. Then, during that night's Twelve Slays of Christmas, he'd made these crazy-insightful comments about the mystery novel. About the trauma of World War I veterans in Dorothy Sayers's book, about what it means for our modern day, and about several other works by the author.

Talk about overachiever vibes—he had them all, and I was completely smitten by them.

And by him?

But I'd only been around him a few times!

I couldn't possibly be falling already. Could I?

Okay, I could.

And my increasingly late nights of texting back and forth with him about random subjects—from Christmas traditions to old TV shows to the future of elevators and cold cereal—proved my precipitous fall.

When I said I hadn't *seen* him in five days, that didn't mean we hadn't communicated. He'd been present for me day and night. Taking up all my free-time thoughts, and a few of my professional-time ones as well.

Seriously, I'd never texted anyone so often in such a short period of time as I had Grant. We hadn't even been on a date, and I was acting all gaga over him, while desperately trying to keep hearts from floating in my eyes wherever I went these days.

Yes, he might be everybody's type—but the more the layers of Grant peeled back, the more he revealed himself to be my type. Precisely.

And the more I wished I could be the one he would finally choose as *his* type.

Even though he knew nothing about my career—and had only seen me while wearing stupid hats.

Well, I only had to wait a few hours now. We had plans this evening.

And maybe the next day, and the next—at least by text, if not in person.

I craved seeing him in person.

Then, it would be Thursday again! My favorite day of the week. Not only did I get to drink Freya's delicious hot chocolate, and talk in depth about books with people who cared as much about stories as did the Guernsey Literary and Potato Peel Pie Society, but I'd also get to see Grant's literature-dissecting mind at work. Sit close to him near the fire. Bask in his presence, refill my Grant cup.

Yep, I had developed a serious crush.

Are we still on for plans for tonight? I needed to know since I hadn't heard from him most of the day, and we hadn't solidified anything. In normal life, I'd beg off, too tired to go on a date.

But this was Grant.

Do you want to go to the holiday kickoff parade with me? My mom needs someone to ride on the Calhoun family parade float. You'd have to dress up. I couldn't tell her no when she asked, but you totally don't have to do this. We can just meet when it's over.

Seriously? That sounded so fun.

I'm there. Where will I find you? I couldn't have him pick me up at the lodge, since I told him I'd be downgrading to a B&B this week. But I was game. *What do I wear?*

Something warm. It's going to snow again.

It's Wilder River. It's always going to snow.

Do you want me to bring an afghan? I can't wait to see you. Head over to the parking lot of the lodge.

With each blink of the text, a new flare of the Northern Lights surged up in the night sky of my soul. Dark green, magenta, purple. The radiant flares lit me up from the inside out.

He couldn't wait to see me!

All the goosebumps. I glanced around for a coat, but caught myself in the mirror. My hair and makeup were still all Glossified.

A date! A date! A date with Grant Calhoun. Should I de-Gloss?

Bitsy came in. "What's with the inner glow? You've been a lantern all week."

"The elevation is probably good for me. And the makeup artist might be working with new techniques and products—for the snow shoots." I couldn't tell her I had a date—especially not with a local. "I'm just taking off my makeup." Good thing Bitsy had come in and pulled me back down to earth. I couldn't have anyone recognizing me.

The taxi driver and Ivory Keyes had been bad enough. Really, I should tell Bitsy.

But Ivory was also afraid of me, so she'd probably keep a Sanna-sighting to herself. Especially if her ex was—by all appearances—dating Sanna.

Ivory wouldn't like looking dumped for someone more famous.

"Elevation. Right. Let me see that text."

I flipped my phone face down.

"You're dating someone."

"Nope." I was totally dating someone. "Okay, but it's new, and I'm being cautious. He's smart and likes to read the same books I do."

Plus, I could've sworn the look in his eyes last time we were together on Thursday night had been more than just attraction.

In the sum of all those moments at the library and then at the book club, and afterwards outside together, and during our obsessive texting, I could've sworn I was seeing the real Grant. The shields-down vulnerable part of him. Plus, the noble, mom-loving, brainy side of him. The funny side. The protective side.

All the sides were turning me into a full-on Grant Calhoun worshiper.

"Okay, but be careful."

"It's all right. He's a good guy. He won't hurt my heart." I didn't know that for certain, but—

"No, I mean, *be careful and don't let anyone from Wilder River know Gloss is shooting commercials starring Sanna.*"

Oh. That kind of careful.

Chapter 12

Grant

"Wilder River loves their Christmas parades." I walked shoulder to shoulder with Roxanna toward the Calhoun family holiday parade entry at the parking lot of the ski lodge. "There are two big ones. First, this kickoff, which goes *down* the main street. Then, next week, it starts down below Sleigh Bells Chalet and works its way up toward the ski lodge. Every float is decked out with all the lights a generator can handle."

"Sounds kinda loud."

"Oh, it is." I couldn't help laughing. "And what's more, the more ambitious parade-float makers add an extra dose of noise by blasting holiday tunes to cover up the grinding of the diesel generators." We bumped shoulders. "It's very festive."

"It sounds totally cheerful."

Actually, it was. And to hear that a sophisticated woman like Roxanna didn't think we were a hick-town bunch of Christmas-obsessed weirdoes made it even better.

"Here's the Calhoun family entry." I rounded the corner to the back-alley placement behind Quality Jewelers where Mom said it would be, and my heart clunked. "Um, looks like it's a royal theme this year for the family float. Is that the Dairy Queen symbol but with the name Calhoun inside?" Near the truck-end of the float were two huge, gilded thrones with red velvet upholstery and ermine capes draped over them. "I'm so sorry."

"Don't be." She went up and draped one of the robes over her shoulders. "It's hilarious to me. I love a quirky sense of humor. My family never did fun stuff like this."

"Are you sure?" I accepted the other robe from her, sweeping it around me. "The Calhoun sense of humor really takes some stretches of goodwill to appreciate."

"Is anyone else coming, or do we get the crowns and capes to ourselves?"

No one else had showed up from the Calhoun cacophony, named so by my late dad. "Who knows."

"These are cool." Roxanna held up two enormous papier mâché crowns that matched the red of the velvet on the thrones—poufy with ermine-looking rims. "You're the king." She placed it on my head and then curtseyed.

"Which makes you the queen." I placed the other crown on her head and then bowed low—until I realized what *king and queen* implied—that we were ... married.

Both of us stiffened, and I'm pretty sure I wore the same shocked look on my face she wore on hers. I took off my crown, and she took off hers. We set them gawkily on the separate thrones.

Moving a little too fast there, even for the mad-dash my heart seemed to be taking.

"Even if you and I get the joke, we're going to garner blank stares from the people watching." I could've wrung Mom's neck. Plus, no other Calhouns were around to diffuse the weirdness. I looked up and down the street, still awkward. "I hope a couple of my cousins show up here. They could at least bring something to pass out to the parade-goers that will make this parade entry make sense."

"Like what?"

"I have no idea." Even as I spoke the words, I knew it wasn't happening. Not even Danica and Jeremy would come to our rescue with a bag of saltwater taffy.

"How much time do we have until the parade starts?" Roxanna asked.

The clock tower at the ski resort struck four thirty. "About half an hour."

Roxanna's eye twinkled. "I have an idea."

***

Thirty minutes later, the parade launched, and the Calhoun float—pulled behind my cousin Eric's pickup truck—lurched into motion. Ahead of us in the parade, a blur of twinkle-lit trailers and old cars blazed a trail with music and honking horns.

But thanks to Roxanna's stroke of genius, the Calhoun's royal float commanded all the applause.

"Hail to the Dairy Queen!" I called out, and to anyone who obeyed, I reached out and offered them an ice cream sandwich. "Three cheers for the Dairy Queen!"

A couple of blocks down the road, she switched places with me, and I was the Dairy King—and she did the royal herald bit. "The Dairy King wishes to bestow Christmas cheer upon all his loyal subjects. Give him your applause."

Roxanna and I had cleared out every shelf in the grocery store—and in a couple of convenience stores. But in the end, we had enough ice cream sandwiches, creamsicles, and frozen sundae cones to last us the entire parade.

"There's one ice cream sandwich left in the final box." She shook it lightly and then offered the open box to me. "Want it?"

"We can share it, if you like."

For a second, she rocked back, as if either recoiling from sharing or recoiling from calories. But then she softened. "I guess half an ice cream won't hurt. Just this once."

I unwrapped it, and broke it in half. She ate her portion greedily, and then closed her eyes, exhaling as if the experience were both completely foreign and completely satisfying.

"Oh, Grant. That was so great."

"The parade, or the ice cream?" *Or being with me?*

"All of it." She opened her eyes, and a soft smile spread over her pretty face. A small smudge of chocolate sandwich remained on the edge of her lip.

"May I?" I asked, holding up my hand. Lightly, I brushed it away. As my finger touched her face, her eyes fluttered shut.

My heart fluttered to life.

She did something to me.

"I have an early morning," she said. "This was more fun than I've had in ages, Grant."

"Can we do it again? Tomorrow night?"

"There's another parade?" she asked, surprised.

"Not *this* week, next. But I meant you and me. Can we do *this* again tomorrow night?"

Her eyes met mine, and she gave a sweet little nod.

We're dating.

"I'll go home now." She went up on tiptoe and her warm lips brushed my cheek. "I'll see you tomorrow."

The kiss shook me to my core. I reverberated with it, like I'd touched a live wire for a split second.

She walked off toward wherever she was staying, her hips swaying slightly, keeping me riveted. I reached into my pocket to pull out my phone. I had to compose a witty text, entertain her, make her smile the second she arrived in her room, so she would go to sleep with thoughts of only me. Hmm. What should I say to charm her, to be the sugarplum that danced in her head?

"Excuse me?" A shrill voice cut the night. "You're playing with fire, Grant. You know that, right?"

Ivory. I steeled my nerve and turned to look at her. "What do you want, Ivory?"

"I want to warn you. As a friend. Stay away from that woman. You don't know anything about her."

Chapter 13

Roxanna

Tuesday evening, I met Grant for dinner at The Hot Chocolate Shop. We discussed Sherlock Holmes—at first. Then, we talked about funny experiences we'd had in high school. He was humble, talking about his stellar sports achievements, always attributing the success to the coach or the team—and blaming the clumsy moments on himself. I told him about my overachiever Hermione Granger-level obsession with grades. He seemed so much more well-rounded than I'd been back then. It inspired me.

The night ended too soon.

Wednesday evening, he ended up staying late at work. Where did he work, anyway? I knew he was a chemist, but where in Wilder River needed a chemist? It was funny—we were getting to know each other very well on a deeper level, but we hadn't covered the small-talk bases.

Frankly, it was nice.

That night we texted late enough into the wee hours that Domingo scolded me for bags under my eyes on Thursday morning at the photo shoot.

"Sorry," I said. "You can use a softer filter, right?" Because I had no intention of curtailing my all-nighters with Grant via phone.

They were filling my soul—breathing new life into me. It felt like a gift I'd always stared at in a catalog, but which I'd never dared hope for. In return, I ached to give Grant what he needed.

I might not know perfectly, but my guess was he needed to be repaired of the damage Ivory had done to him.

I wanted to be the woman to give him that healing gift.

Thursday night came at last—book club, where it felt like I couldn't sit close enough to him on the love-seat by the fire. The Sherlock Holmes discussion blurred past my ears. I did offer a few comments, but even my own voice sounded like Charlie Brown's teacher to me, I was so caught up in Grant, Grant, Grant.

When it was over, I stood up, and leaving his side felt like an amputation. That energetic connection to his touch was so invigorating.

"I'll take you home?" Grant walked out the door with me, holding both our copies of the Father Brown mystery by G. K. Chesterton. "I feel like we haven't seen each other lately."

Same! "I'd like that, but I already arranged a taxi." It waited across the snowy parking lot. "But thank you. Please tell Dasher hi from me." I rushed to the taxi before Grant could argue. No one in Wilder River could find out where I was staying—thanks to Gordon Gloss's insistence in the contract, which I'd signed. "I'll watch for your texts, though!" I hollered as I climbed inside.

He nodded, raising a hand, looking confused. And a little rejected.

I flipped my phone over and waited for his text. It came before the taxi driver arrived at the only stoplight in town.

Date. Tomorrow night. Seven. Wear something warm. It wasn't even a request—it was a demand.

Something in me liked it, a lot. It felt possessive, but in a good way.

We didn't text that night. We had the following evening to look forward to.

The next morning, during hair and makeup, I basked in the glowing letters of his text again.

"Well, well. Who's asking you on a date?" Bitsy peeked over my shoulder at my phone.

91

"Bitsy." I turned my phone over, but my palm pulsed against it. "You're reading my texts again."

She ignored my accusation. "Don't tell me it's *actually* Mr. T asking you out."

For a second, her question didn't compute. Oh, right. The screen name I'd given him—*Mr. T* in my contact list stood for *Mr. Thirteen-on-a-Scale-of-Ten.* "What do you think?"

"Hmm. You with the 1980s boxing and TV star with all the gold chains? He's way too old for you, believe me. The paparazzi would have a heyday—Sanna and the man who made the West-African Mandinka warrior haircut famous."

"Yep, too old. But still a very cool dude."

She tapped my shoulder with a can of GlossTastic aerosol hairspray. "Tell him yes, Roxanna," the stylist said with a gleam in her eye. "Remind him he's a lucky guy."

"I might." Except, he already knew I was going with him. I hadn't even needed to respond.

Bitsy followed on. "Take a chance. He might be different from all the others in the past."

"You mean, the guys who were after Sanna? Believe it or not, he has no idea what my job is."

Bitsy dropped the GlossTastic setting spray. The lid popped off and rolled one direction while the can rolled in the other. "Don't tell me he's local and you've been sneaking out and meeting people!"

"Why would you suspect that?"

"Because"—she waved the can in a circle—"I have a brain. I pity the fool that doesn't."

"Nice Mr. T reference." Still, how did she know? I came clean. "Okay, he's local, but I'm being careful. I promise."

Bitsy's lips twisted. "Gloss absolutely wants this filming kept under wraps."

That sobered me. She left, and I flipped my phone back over. The text still glowed. Grant's laugh and smile replaced those thoughts, softening my soul into room-temperature butter.

Friday afternoon, just before evening light faded past ideal for filming, Domingo the director took me aside. "I thought of you as the consummate professional model before, but today? Sanna, you gave me something extra special. There was a sparkle that the camera picked up and captured, and this—*this*—is the million-dollar footage. Thank you. It's an honor." He took my hand and kissed the back of it. "Whatever you're doing to create that glow, keep it up."

I'm falling in love with Grant Calhoun, that's what.

Chapter 14

Grant

Date night! I'd see Roxanna in an hour. I spun in a circle that knocked my safety glasses askew.

"Watch it, or you'll knock the chemicals into the Bunsen burner, and we'll all be roasted like chestnuts." Zed stood at the door of the lab, and his words brought me to a halt. "You take up whirling-Dervish lessons while I was you-know-where, or something?"

"Did you get the Panukaa oil?" I shoved my phone in my lab coat pocket, but I'd pull it out and look at Roxanna's and my texting threads again later. Savor them. Get drunk on them. Like I was acting now. "I've been using plain old coconut oil, and soybean oil, and some other standard ingredients as a Panukaa oil substitute in my work the past two weeks, and nothing has been as effective. So, hand it over."

Zed frowned. "It was a bust."

My pulse raced. "Uh, what do you mean?" He had to have sourced it. We needed it!

"I mean, I got to the farm, and the farmer gave me a helpless shrug. He'd just signed with another company that had bought all stock on hand—plus the full crop for the following three years."

My gut twisted. "That's—you should've called me." What were we going to do now?

"I tried, but you know how far up in the wilds of New Zealand that farm was."

Good point. "Well, is there any *good* news?" I could use a counterbalance to this devastation that made my head swirl.

"Unfortunately, no. In fact, I'm here to bring even worse news. We need the final formula ready for production by the fifteenth of December."

Gut punch! "But—but I thought you said Christmas." I could've doubled over, gasping.

"They moved it up—for me, actually."

I balked. "Why for you?" That seemed strange, to change things for the head marketer, when everything else had a strict timeline. Including me. "Is something ..."

"Dallin."

Oh, Dallin. His son. "Is he—?"

"Actually, that's the only great news." Zed sort of smiled, as though the *great* part of the news came with a heaping tablespoon of *not-so-great.* "His surgery is finally scheduled. The transplant is coming available right before Christmas."

"Right." I couldn't allow myself to complain, considering I could never imagine what it was like to be in his shoes. "The fifteenth it is!" After all the effort he'd made, leaving Pamela to care for Dallin and the rest of the Fearsome Five, too. He really was dedicated to this company. His whole family had sacrificed. *Like mine.* "Thanks for trying to get the originally planned supplies. I'll figure something out—fast. And it will be even better. In fact, this could be a great thing." Right? "Tell Pamela thanks for being a trooper."

"I will. Thanks for being so cool about it." Zed gave me a slap on the back. "Hee-haw." He used the same phrase as George Bailey's best friend, Sam, on *It's a Wonderful Life.*

You're still missing the formula, the Gandalf in my head hollered.

No duh, Gandalf. It doesn't take a wizard to know that.

"The deadline is my fault, so I'll do whatever I can to help." Zed looked around. "We'd better be fast—faster than Gloss. That's all

Bolton and the upstairs people are asking, or they're talking about cuts, Grant. All kinds of them. So, *beat Gloss*."

"Beat Gloss," I said, raising a fist of solidarity.

As soon as Zed left the lab, my arm dropped heavily at my side.

Gloss, Gloss, Gloss. *Not today, Gloss*.

Nope. For now, I had a date with Roxanna Reid. Gloss threats wouldn't distract me from anticipating the pleasure of her honeysuckle scent. River Tresses would have none of my attention tonight at the second holiday lights parade.

Mmm. Honeysuckle. Roxanna Reid made my veins run with honey.

Sure, I should have probably waited until my formula was complete before dating her, but I craved her.

She's a Christmas present you're opening early. Gandalf's chuckle reverberated in my mind. *Holiday magic infuses you.*

Oh, brother. That wizard brain voice needed to halt.

Tonight was our third official date. With any luck, I would be kissing her tonight. That pout had been begging me to ever since we met.

"You're leaving already?" Lucy carried the crate of glass bottles toward the supply room. "It's barely five."

"It's dark. It's the weekend. We stayed past midnight on Wednesday. I'm heading out."

"I notice you didn't say you're going home." Lucy lifted that accusing brow at me. "It's that girl, isn't it?"

Why lie? "Her name is Roxanna Reid. We have a lot in common."

"Did you say Roxanna Reid?" Lucy tilted her head.

My phone chimed a text. *Can I meet you somewhere?* Roxanna!

"Sorry, Lucy." I shrugged out of my lab coat and grabbed my long wool coat and scarf. "Gotta go. The parade starts in an hour." And I wanted to get dinner with Roxanna first. And then, maybe hold her hand during the parade. And after? Well, after, I wanted to spend some quality time with Roxanna away from book club members, away from parade-goers. Just Roxanna's exquisite brown eyes gazing up into mine, her chin uplifted, her soft lips parting slightly …

"Grant?" Lucy broke my spell. "Have a good weekend."

I intended to. Fully.

I'll pick you up. I texted back as I rode the elevator up to the ground floor from the basement-level where the lab was. *Where's good?*

I'm at the ski lodge. I'll meet you in the circle.

The Wilder River Lodge? Had she been skiing today? Good for her. I loved skiing when I had time. Maybe she and I could ski together after the snowpack came. Or take the toboggan run before it snowed. Yeah, tobogganing with her would be great, with my arms wrapped around her waist, the honey of her hair and skin in my senses.

"Grant?" Kringle, the night watchman at River Tresses, who played Santa every year at the company Christmas parties based on both his name and his size, stood outside the open elevator doors. "You getting off the elevator? Or going back down?"

I looked up from my phone. Great. My mind had better focus at least long enough to drive safely to the ski lodge to pick her up. Otherwise, I'd crash and burn literally and figuratively.

***

"Have you been waiting long?" I held open the door of my old white truck for her. Suddenly, it didn't look like the golden chariot I'd always considered it to be. Sure, it'd been good enough for Dasher and me, for the rakes and shovels I needed at Mom's yard, but Roxanna deserved better. She deserved the best. "Did you hit the slopes today?" I said as I drove toward the restaurant.

She tilted her head at me, as if hunting for a response. "I hiked up them a little."

Roxanna and me on a hike, along with Dasher, taking in the view of the river valley. Taking her in my arms, and …

Dang. I was crushing hard, and the discombobulation raged. "Is it okay if we go to the Christmas Hamper street festival? No parade, but

97

instead, vendors light up their booths. You walk down the street and choose items for a Christmas Eve Hamper to share with someone as charity or for someone you love."

"Of course! That sounds great. But what's a Christmas Eve Hamper?"

I explained the town's tradition—stolen from England's tradition—of filling a lidded basket with surprises to open on Christmas Eve, like pajamas and treats and movie popcorn.

"That's really nice," she said. "And you buy from local artisans for this? What a great way to support everyone—givers and creators and receivers alike."

"Yeah." I loved how she thought.

We drove downtown. She rested her hand beside her leg on the bench seat of the truck. I took it as an invitation and reached over and laced my fingers through hers.

My hand pulsated as much as when our palms had touched that first time we met. Touching her seemed so obvious, so natural a state of things, after all the communication we'd done over the past week.

Our texting threads danced in my head—sweet and nostalgic. We'd discussed everything and nothing. Elementary school memories. Fishing trips. Her friend Danica being married to my cousin Jeremy. The weight of my always being contrasted with Jeremy's reputation growing up. The weight of her never having a mom in the home to guide her.

I felt like I knew Roxanna at her core more than any of the Ivory-types I'd ever dated. The real Roxanna.

Which was strange, since we hadn't done *any* of the basic small talk. She didn't even know where I worked, nor did I know about her job, other than the fact she was a grad student studying English literature. Maybe her work was a research project for literature.

Regardless, the sheer *rightness* of her touch made none of that matter to me.

My stomach growled like a bear.

"Have you eaten?" I asked and steered my truck down a side street. "Do you like grilled cheese sandwiches?" We soon rolled up to the best diner on planet Earth. "Welcome to the best grilled cheese of your life."

"I adore grilled cheese. You'd have to be broken on some cosmic level to dislike grilled cheese."

I helped her down from the truck. "They also have really good apple pie."

"Ooh, I love apple pie. It's been a decade." Her shoulder bumped against my bicep as we walked toward the diner's entrance.

"Since you had really good apple pie, or since you had apple pie?"

"Uh-huh."

"How can you be missing out on a key ingredient of the good life like apple pie?" There was that Gandalf phrase again: *key ingredient.* It kept popping up. I shushed Gandalf again. He wouldn't be playing third-wheel on this date. *I'm on a date with Roxanna. Back off, pal. Give us some privacy.* "We'll fix that tonight."

Clouds hung low and threatening, and flakes descended onto the piles of snow that had accumulated the day before.

Inside, I ordered four classic grilled cheese sandwiches and four pieces of pie—two for each of us. Plus, a chocolate shake for me and a vanilla shake for her. They came first, topped with whipped cream and a maraschino cherry.

"Have you ever tried doing this?" Roxanna popped the whole cherry into her mouth, and a few seconds later, she popped the stem out—tied in a knot.

"How did you do that?" I couldn't take my eyes off her tongue.

"Magic." She smiled, as Gandalf chortled. "And practice."

Oh, if she'd practice that magic on me.

"You didn't eat all of your pie." In fact, she'd only eaten half of one piece of pie, and half of one of her grilled cheese sandwiches. "Did you pre-eat before our date?" Girls I'd dated in the past had done that. *It's a red flag.* "You never need to do that around me. Just, you know, be yourself."

For a long moment, she stared at me with those deep brown eyes, a look of debate in them. Finally she said, "Thanks." She took another half of a grilled cheese and bit off the pointy corner. "I appreciate that."

Still, she didn't eat the rest, and she offered me her second piece of pie. I wolfed it down.

After dinner, we headed back to Main Street for the Christmas Hamper vendor show.

Crowds thronged. We paused at the first booth, where a woman dressed as a fluffy, rotund Mrs. Claus handed us a Christmas Hamper to fill. "Fill it to the brim. If you do, your heart will be just as full." She smiled, her round cheeks red with blush.

"This is so fun, Grant. Who should we give our hamper to?"

I knew. "My friend from work has a son who's getting surgery right before Christmas."

"Perfect. How old is he?"

"Ten." I knew Dallin's age, as he and I shared a birthday, and he was exactly twenty-five years younger than I was. "And he's obsessed with farm animals. He wants to grow up and run a ranch with sheep and cattle. He showed a lamb in the county fair this fall."

"He sounds great. I hope I get to be the mom of a great kid like that."

"My buddy is lucky and he knows it." My heart pinched. The world would be a worse place without Dallin. "Let's see what they've got."

We strolled up the street, stopping at booths here and there. We found a curry comb with a candy cane-striped handle, perfect for Dallin's pony. Next, we chose some electrically heated thermal socks.

"These would be great for hospital stays." Roxanna put them in the hamper. "Feet get cold there, I hear."

I pictured her mom in the hospital after giving birth to a beautiful, dark-eyed baby, cold feet, trying to hang on to life. *Poor Roxanna. No mom.* Too bad I couldn't share mine. My mom was enough mom for ten people.

Santa Claus—Kringle, the security guard from River Tresses—chuckled and waved from a giant, light-bedecked sleigh as he handed out bags of candy. We added one to our hamper.

"Ho, ho, ho!" Kringle batted my shoulder as I reached for the candy bag. "Looks like you already got your Christmas present, town hero." His eye twinkled.

I could've popped him right in the kisser. "Merry Christmas," I said through clenched teeth instead.

"Town hero?" Roxanna asked as we edged away, stuffing the candy bag into the already full hamper.

"Hardly. I'm just a lowly chemist, working to make Wilder River a better place." I took her hand. Her honey scent washed over me, effectively shutting out all other sensations. She was intoxicating.

"Your Great-Grandpa Richard Grant Wilder would be proud of you." She squeezed my hand, and my heart kind of exploded.

One darted glance down at her, and I was a goner. I had to get her alone, kiss her, show her what she was starting to mean to me. No, what she already meant to me.

"So, Roxanna?" I asked, looking for an easy way to escape, a way to turn her down a side street, get her alone. "I think we have enough stuff for the hamper." It was full to overflowing now. "Should we—"

"Sanna!" A teenage girl ran up to us, whipped out her phone, and took a picture of Roxanna. "It's you! I heard you were in Wilder River, but I didn't think I'd see you in real life. Everyone! It's Sanna!"

Roxanna ducked behind me. The sides and sleeves of my coat went tight, as if she were gripping them for dear life.

Sanna? What did that mean?

"Excuse me." I smiled at the teenager. "I'm afraid you have my girlfriend confused with someone else."

Had I just announced to a stranger that Roxanna was my girlfriend? *I had.*

And it feels so right, doesn't it? Flipping Gandalf. Fine. It did.

Just like her nearness behind me—practically glued to my spine—

felt good.

However, the girl was still crowding us, and some of her friends were gathering.

"I can't believe I get to see Sanna!" She swooned.

"Excuse me, but could you please take a step back?"

"Grant Calhoun?" Her voice came out breathy—in a way I'd heard a hundred times before from women. "Hi. Are you really here with Sanna? I'm dying. This is a perfect combination for holiday love. Could I please get a selfie? I'll pay. I'll—" Her voice skewed into desperation, maybe a little manic.

Yikes.

"Grant." Roxanna's voice was muffled since she'd buried her face in my coat. "Can we get out of here? Fast? I don't feel safe."

"You don't have to ask me twice." I'd been dying for time alone with this gorgeous woman.

"Ready?" I twisted around, the hamper swinging from the crook of my elbow, and scooped Roxanna up in my arms. I carried her into the nearest alley, moving fast. For a minute, footfalls dogged us, or so I imagined.

Roxanna, with her face still buried in my coat, said, "Grant! Watch out for slick spots!"

Night had fallen, and now that we were away from the town's parade lights, it seemed dark and deserted.

I jogged on, holding her close, breathing her scent. We came to the next street. Paused at the curb was none other than the horse-drawn carriage of the Sleigh Bells Chalet. "Lenny?" I waved him down. "Are you supposed to be taking people for rides at the vendor event?"

I set Roxanna down, but she clung to me, as if still hiding and terrified.

Lenny aimed a thumb over his shoulder. "I already finished the route. I was waiting for traffic to clear out before I take Donner and Blitzen back to the stable. You want to go somewhere, Grant?"

"A sleigh ride? Really? Oh, look, it's all covered with lights!"

Roxanna asked, after finally peeking out from my chest. She'd sparkled when she'd first heard about a sleigh ride, back when we first met Ellery and Bing Whitmore, owners of the hotel and sleigh. The sight of the sleigh seemed to erase her fear.

Lenny shrugged. "Well, it has wheels instead of runners, so it's more of a wagon ride than a sleigh ride until I get the runners put on. Been busy with the hotel. It's so packed for the Christmas Hamper event and all."

While it wouldn't get us alone, it would get us away. "We'd love a ride—*away* from the crowds, if possible."

"Nothing would make Donner and Blitzen happier. They're keyed up and tugging like they need a canter, so this is helpful for them and me, actually."

I handed Roxanna up into the sleigh and then sat down beside her. Lenny pulled out a quilt and handed it over to us, our necks snapping backward with the G-forces as Donner and Blitzen took off.

"It's a serious ride!" Roxanna nestled close to me. "And freezing."

"True!" I spread the cozy blanket from the seat of the sleigh over our laps. She slid so close to my side I could practically share a pulse with her. I wrapped an arm around her waist, pulling her even closer. It felt righter than right.

"This is amazing, Grant." Roxanna tilted her chin back and looked up at the night sky. "The clouds are glowing."

So was I.

The town's streetlights and homes lit up the sky, but Roxanna lit me.

"Thanks for making a fast exit." She looked up at me, her face finally relaxing from the tension that had been there since we'd first spotted Lenny and made our escape.

"What do you think that girl's problem was?"

Lenny's sleigh emerged on the far side of town, near the old Victorian homes section. "Is this good?" Lenny asked.

"Sure," I said. "We can just go for a walk now. Thanks, man." I gave him a few bills from my wallet.

"Thanks, Grant. Anything to help Wilder River's MVP." He doffed his cap at us and then drove on, the sleigh bells jingling and the lights around the sleigh winking out after he crested the hill.

"Wilder River's MVP?" Roxanna snuggled up against my arm. "Pressure much?"

"A guy does what he can." If I could get the formula right, I'd save the River Tresses plant and all the jobs from the impending Gloss threats.

Threats of takeover.

Because that was what loomed, right? Even though I was no longer part of the upstairs administration team at River Tresses, I'd been there. The thrust of all Zed's warnings was clear.

If I could save the plant, Grandfather Wilder's work to build the town would live on. Otherwise, his legacy could die off entirely.

"You can do whatever you set your mind to, Grant. I believe in you."

Strength infused me. Light, and warmth, and truth. Roxanna infused me.

I turned toward her. *I have to kiss her.* I leaned in, and—

Lights of a front porch flooded the air around us.

"Look at that house!" Roxanna gaped. We'd climbed out of the sleigh in front of a two-story pink Victorian with a tower. Peppermint Drop Inn, if I remembered right. Nice wraparound porch. Pretty fountains. "It's everything!" she breathed.

Everything except the privacy I was seeking. The kissing chance was gone. For now.

But not forever.

"You like it?"

"Of course! Who wouldn't? Well, other than someone who rejects beauty and style."

"Or hates pink."

"That, but even pink-rejecters would be more charmed than they'd admit, I'm sure."

I was more charmed than I could admit. "Should we ask for a tour?"

"They give them?"

"Maybe not at night." I took her hand. Our palms pressed together, and it was like I'd had a three-cup caffeine hit. My senses all sped up. "If you stick around in Wilder River, we could arrange one, for sure. You're just working here for ... how long?"

I shouldn't pry, since she never asked about my work, and it almost seemed like she was purposely avoiding the topic. Did it bother me that there were some things she hadn't shared with me? I wasn't sure. I sensed some secrets existed—and very literally my visual sense homed in on a glaring kept-secret every time we were together. Tonight, instead of that cat hat, or the poufy beret, she wore a lumpy stocking beanie. Not much better.

To be blunt, in all the times we'd met, she hadn't ever revealed her hair. One stray lock of chestnut, and that was all.

Why not? It didn't bug me—but if this went on, it might start to. After all, I spent all my days thinking about how different chemical combinations affected the health of human hair. It was basically my current obsession.

Were there other secrets? She'd mentioned a rift with her father, hinted at it without explaining more. I'd spilled all that baggage about my ancestor, Richard Grant Wilder, described my biggest motivation in life as saving the town. Meanwhile, Roxanna was a mostly closed book by comparison.

If not deep secrets, what was she willing to share? Anything? Because I couldn't settle for the shallow end anymore. I'd dated too much in the shallows. Roxanna's waters ran deep. Would she let me in?

We'd walked a few paces down the street, away from Peppermint Drop Inn, and near a copse of trees that had lost their leaves.

"Tell me something about yourself." I placed my hand around her waist again. "Something meaningful."

It was more than bold, but I craved a deeper connection with her. I had to know whether I could allow myself to keep falling for her.

Frankly, the cat hat and her hair secret paled in comparison to knowing who she truly was and why.

I faced her, and her baby-deer eyes widened as she looked up at me. Her lips parted, and she moistened them. I could kiss them instantly, but I might miss something far more important.

Would she answer? I couldn't breathe.

"It's my dad." Her brows pushed together. "He's why I would never read mystery novels. He's why I think it's bunk that justice is always served. Or, well, why it cuts like all the daggers in all the cloak-and-dagger spy thrillers." Her voice was raw and ragged.

"Did he … commit a crime?" My thoughts blared—*Did he kill someone?* Murder mysteries would definitely explain why she was upset in the library last week while reading Dorothy Sayers, if so.

"Don't look so horrified. Yes, he committed a crime, but nothing violent."

I exhaled. For her sake more than my own. "That's rough." My worry must have shown.

"It was a white-collar crime." She blew out a breath and launched. "About ten years ago, he defrauded the corporation he worked for. He got away with it for a while. We were rich. Or so I thought. Then, they caught on to him. When he hired a defense attorney, I foolishly assumed that meant he was defending his innocence. I cried for him, defended him to all my friends at school who'd heard about him on the news and from their parents. I shouted that my dad was innocent."

"He wasn't," I confirmed, gravely.

"He wasn't." She grimaced. "They took him to prison on Christmas Eve. Christmas Eve! It crushed me. Not so much because the judge found him guilty, but because, after all the work of the attorneys, he ended up changing his plea to guilty. Upon which, the judge ordered him to pay attorneys' fees for both sides." Her face tightened. "I have been working ever since then to make things right to those he victimized. I sold our house. Our cars. Even Yeti, my beautiful Samoyed."

She looked sick. I felt sick for her.

"Was it enough?" I could tell, though. It hadn't been enough. My belly filled with compassion for this woman who was nothing like any other woman I'd ever met. "And you're still working hard to fix things?" She shouldn't be! Legal fees were his responsibility, not hers.

Wow, and I thought *I* had a heavy legacy.

"I am. I work at a job I'm qualified for and love, but which doesn't put me on the path toward teaching. My mom would've wanted me to teach. Worse, I had to postpone getting the rest of my schooling while I got my temporary career established in order to pay for Dad's mistakes."

That stunk. For a criminal father, she had to keep putting off her higher calling in life. "Is the end in sight?"

"Every time I think I am close, the goal posts seem to move." She shook her head. "I repaid the plaintiffs' lawyers two years ago, and by working here in Wilder River on assignment, my hope is that by Christmas I can fork over the final payment to Dad's lawyer." She muttered something, and I thought I heard the phrase *thorn in my side.* "It would be the best Christmas present to myself I could imagine."

"Roxanna." I gathered her into my arms. "You are a good daughter." Just like I wanted to be a good son and great-grandson. "You gave up Yeti to repair your dad's integrity. That must have been a sacrifice."

She looked up at me. "You think so? You think I'm a good daughter?"

It wasn't the sensual lead-up I'd allowed myself to envision. It wasn't like the first kiss between Captain Vartigan and the Rygraff Queen, or like any book I'd read.

Instead, it was just a beautiful woman, who believed I was worthy of love and of my ancestor's approval, in my arms. And she needed my validation and approval. She was pressing her softness against my torso, her breath whispering against my cheek like a soft breeze, and her deep brown eyes beckoning me forward, forward, forward.

I obeyed that tug. The kiss was a living thing, a force of its own. I succumbed to its siren call.

When our lips met at last, her sweetness infused me, luscious and floral. It had to be the most delicious thing that had ever happened to anyone ever.

I sipped the kiss's nectar cautiously at first. Then, when she responded with a soft sigh, I came undone. Suddenly, I was drinking deeply from Roxanna's lips and her kiss. A parched intergalactic traveler on a desert planet who'd unexpectedly discovered the fountain of life.

Roxanna reached around and placed her hands on my back, giving gentle pressure, and my hands found her hips, resting there but tugging her close.

It was like adding the final ingredient to a formula—the one where several inert ingredients had lain latent in the test tube, and then suddenly, *catalytic agent!* Our kiss was an overflowing chemistry, filling the whole laboratory of my soul. And it smelled and tasted of honey.

Honey, honey, honey. Every pass of her lips spun the sugar of my soul. I couldn't drink deeply enough, couldn't stop wanting more and more of this delicious moment.

She wasn't just the key ingredient—she was the key.

Chapter 15

Roxanna

Kisses light and feathery alternated with kisses desperately anxious and passionate. I could kiss him for an hour. For a lifetime.

Kissing Grant Calhoun was a revelation akin to the twist-ending of a classic book's plot. I never saw it coming—the sincerity of his touch, the perfection of his strengths, the vulnerability and hope combining between us physically and emotionally. My every cell responded as he kissed me with what felt like his *true self.*

Unmasked, Grant Calhoun, the man my mind had fallen for, and now the rest of me would be wrecked if his kiss didn't belong to me forevermore.

Another kiss. He thought I was a good daughter. Another kiss. He understood how hard it was to give up my beloved Yeti. Another kiss. He himself valued being a good grandson to that ancestor he revered.

My head and heart and the rest of me instantly knew in the touch of that kiss that Grant Calhoun was the man I'd been unconsciously seeking all my life. One I could believe in. One who wouldn't betray me. One who cared about goodness and justice. With Grant, maybe I could actually start believing the possibility that all those books I'd been reading all my life possibly held real-life meaning. That love and justice and connection could belong *to me.* In reality, not just in fiction.

"I'm falling for you, Grant," I said with a hush. *Hard and fast and completely*, I said silently.

"Isn't it obviously mutual?" he said back. "I can't stop kissing you." Grant's lips left mine to trail heat along my jawline

"Good. Don't." I rose up on tiptoe and kissed him with all the fervor that hummed inside me. His hands moved from my hips to my lower back.

I gathered the back of his coat into my fists, gripping tightly. *Never let go of me, Grant. Never let this moment end.* He kissed my lips, my cheek, my jaw, a place below my ear, and with every placement, I grew more invested.

After a long time but not long enough, he pulled away and looked at me, an intensity flickered in his irises. "Wow, Roxanna. That was …"

"Uh-huh." I buried my face in his chest. "It was."

A cold fleck touched my cheek. And another, and another.

"It's snowing." I managed to verbalize the obvious.

"Just a flurry. Mmm." He didn't seem all that interested in snow. "Roxanna, you're …" He started kissing me again.

However, the flurry changed its mind and turned into a heavy snowfall. Huge clusters of flakes began collecting on our shoulders and heads.

From the fold of his coat's inner pocket, Grant produced an umbrella. He popped it open. "My mom insists I always carry an umbrella. Turns out for once, she wasn't wrong."

"Your mom seems smart." Again, my heart fluttered a little at the thought of a man who cared about and respected his mother.

"She is smart. Maybe we should head back."

He held the umbrella over both of us with his left hand, but with his right hand, he grasped my hand and stuck both our hands into his warm coat pocket. There, he laced our fingers, pressing his palm to mine in a way reminiscent of that electric moment.

"Do you remember when we first shook hands? In the Hot Chocolate Shop?" It was a vulnerable question, but I had to know. "I felt something."

"Yeah. Same," he said. "Did it bring to your mind a nuclear reactor?"

So he'd felt it too? I knew it! I pressed my hand to his more tightly. Who knew there was a direct link between hand and heart?

"The vendor event is over, I'm sure." He guided me around a slushy low spot. "I think we left the hamper in Lenny's sleigh."

"We'll get it sometime." I could pick it up between shoots tomorrow. Or any day. I was in Wilder River for weeks yet, along with Colonel Race, and Miss Marple, and Hercule Poirot—and several other sleuths created by Dame Agatha. All of those minds and characters and adventures paled in comparison to my time with Grant, though.

We watched the snowflakes dancing and drifting under the streetlights as we walked. "What do you think made that girl go so berserk when she saw you?"

Ah, that. It had to come up, eventually. Grant wasn't dumb— definitely. But even the biggest pros about a person's character often contained a con.

"She was so insistent you were famous and named something else. Sanna, she said?"

"Psychosis of some kind, do you think?" I joked, but he called my bluff.

"I don't know as much about you as I feel like I should know." He brushed his hand down my cheek. "This is tiny, but I'm not even sure what color your hair is, which seems like a basic thing to know. You always wear a hat when I see you."

"My hair isn't like Ivory's, if that's what you're worried about."

"I'm not worried about you having *any* resemblance to Ivory. Actually, I thought I saw a dark brown lock of your hair escape once."

More than anything, I longed to pull the hat from my head and let my hair loose. But we were outside, walking down a side street back toward the center of Wilder River. Anyone might see us.

I ached to tell him the truth—at least a portion of it. But how could

111

I, without directly violating my contract? Maybe I should just come out with it. "I have a weird situation that forces me to keep my hair hidden in public."

"Really? That does sound like a weird situation." Grant held my hand as we crossed the street toward his waiting truck. "Are you saying if we had a little time alone together, *not in public,* that it would be different?"

"Maybe, but possibly not. It's hard to explain." My contract specifically prohibited divulging my identity outside the Gloss corporate structure during my time working in Wilder River. But, considering this was Grant, the most principled and trustworthy person I'd ever encountered, there had to be a way around it. "Do you have access to a computer and printer?"

"No printer at home, but I have one at my office." We arrived at Grant's truck, and he helped me into the passenger side. I'd never dated anyone who opened my door for me before.

"Can you take me to your office?" I had an idea.

"Um." He started his truck, and then he waited before putting it in gear, instead gripping the wheel with both hands and looking straight ahead. "It's more like a laboratory with an office attached. Chemicals, all that. I shouldn't really take non-employees there."

"We won't need the lab. We'll only be using a word processor. And just for a few minutes."

"If it's just a word processor, then"—he put his truck in gear—"it's probably all right. You're working on a master's degree in English literature, right? No interest in chemical formulas?" He took a few turns and went up a hill on a side-street so thick with trees I couldn't even see the ski lodge or the town.

"None whatsoever. Chemistry was a fun class, but the last time I studied it, I was seventeen and a junior in high school."

Soon, we entered the darkened parking lot of a large industrial building—Wilder River Lab Company. Grant waved a card at a reader and a gate opened to an underground area. After parking, we took an elevator downward, third subbasement. Wow, he really did work in a serious lab.

"This is cool." I followed him down a tiled hallway, my boots clattering on the floor and echoing. We arrived at the door of his lab, and he unlocked it, but there, he paused.

"Really? You think so?" A light danced in his eyes.

"Completely. I'm a sucker for sparkly stuff, and this place is so clean it gleams." I peeked inside, and he let me enter the room—clinical and shining.

"It doesn't bother you that I'm a chemistry geek?" His tone sounded more vulnerable than I would've expected, considering.

"Your intelligence is one of your most attractive features." I rose up on tiptoe and pulled his forehead toward me to kiss it. "Did you really mean it when you called me your girlfriend earlier?"

Maybe he had only said those words to brush off the superfan.

My confidence faltered slightly, like the ankles of a new skater coming onto the ice. I wanted him to want me so badly.

"Hundred percent. If you'll allow it, that is."

Oh, I'd allow it. I kissed him tenderly, and he returned the affection for another minute, and I sailed all around the lab, seeing nothing and feeling everything—for this Thirteen-on-a-Ten-Scale man who'd definitely been underrated and underappreciated by everyone in the past.

Plus, his kiss wasn't even on the scale.

"Sorry." I tore myself out of the ecstasy. I'd asked him to bring me here to his office for a definite purpose. "I could do that all night, but I want to answer your question. Where's your computer?"

A minute later, I sat at his desk in a little office off the back of the laboratory, typing up a document of employment. "Can I print?"

He showed me how. When it came off the printer, I handed the warm, newly printed contract to Grant.

"Read it? How do the terms sound?"

Grant cleared his throat, and in an amused tone read, "I, Roxanna

Reid, hereby extend employment to Grant Calhoun, to serve as my Location Adviser. He will be compensated in-kind." He looked up, his eye twinkling. "I hope *in-kind* means what I think it means."

I ran a finger across my lower lip. "What do you think it means?"

One side of his mouth went up, and then he kept reading. "The duration of this contract is negotiable and can be terminated by either party. Blah, blah, blah, blah, signed." He reached for a pen, and we both signed on the line.

The second I finished the final letter of my name, I stood up, took off my knitted cap, and shook out my hair. Freedom.

And the shock and enchantment on Grant's face was the payment-in-kind I'd been begging for. I hoped it would cause him to forget to ask what a Location Adviser did and for what job.

"Wow," he breathed. "That's amazing."

My back arched toward him as he took me in his arms again and kissed me deeply.

"Thank you for letting me see you." Another kiss. "You're sweet as honey."

Suddenly, Grant pulled back, dropped his arms, and then gave himself a classic smack on the forehead. "It's there! It's been there the whole time since I met you. The key ingredient!" He scooped me up and swung me around. My heels toppled his desk chair, but he didn't set me down until we started kissing again.

"What is it?" I asked when he kissed my neck. "I'm happy for you, but I'm not following."

"Honey!"

Terms of endearment? Already? We'd just started dating. Kissing. Tonight. "Yes?" I asked, my heart floated. I'd always dreamed of being given a nickname. "Should I call you, babe?"

He pulled back. "What?" He tilted his head. "Oh! No, honey is the key ingredient my formula needs. In fact, it's perfect. Honey has medicinal properties, can heal skin, and nourish. In fact, Mom has been studying bees like they're going out of style. There's a specific honeybee—Apis polaris, which is her personal favorite bee—that pollinates the heather on the tundra in northern Greenland, but someone has imported it to Wilder River and has been using them to farm local honey. Wilder River honey is exactly what I've been looking for! To go with the Wilder River spring water that you inspired me to use in the formula."

"Me?"

"You probably didn't notice, but the first time we met, you asked me if there was something special about the water in Wilder River, at the headwaters, and it triggered a memory. I've been using pure spring water to reinvigorate the original formula, and it's almost there. If I add the Wilder River honey, it's a sure-fire win, with or without the Panukaa oil that Zed couldn't source in New Zealand on his trip." He wore an ecstatic smile—but a look of sharp alarm canceled it, so I quickly interjected to show him how happy I was, too.

"That's great, Grant. I have no idea what Panukaa means, and I don't know what I did to help, but it's fabulous to see you this happy."

But I was mentally rushing back to the benefits of honey. "Plus, since it's basically unknown, we can use local Wilder River honey without other companies competing. It's the missing piece! Combined with the surfactants, Wilder River honey and de-ionized water from Wilder River are the key ingredients! Altogether, they are the synthesis I've been searching for all along. You're the muse, Roxanna!"

He kissed me again, and I sank into the sweetness of his compliments, bathed in his goodness, and sank into the moment of officially being Grant's girlfriend, muse, and confidant.

I'd fallen hard.

Chapter 16

Grant

It took all my willpower to drive Roxanna back to the ski lodge and then to stop kissing her long enough to let her out of my truck. I didn't dare walk her to the door of the lodge for fear I'd go inside and continue showing her how much I was falling for her—past the point of propriety. Roxanna Reid was too precious to treat like she wasn't absolute gold.

Her alchemy had worked gold in me, that was for sure.

I probably shouldn't have uttered the words *Panukaa oil* to her, or mentioned these Wilder River-specific ingredients, but she wouldn't tell anyone about honey or spring water. She was a college student. I was being paranoid. Plus, she trusted me to be her Location Adviser. We were in a formal contract.

Home. I should go home, but my adrenaline buzzed like the bees on all the local wildflowers on the mountainsides—from fireweed, to yarrow, to Indian paintbrush, to spirea, and I rushed to the pharmacy. It stayed open late during the ski season. Would they have Wilder River honey? Mom had said something about Pete selling it in the pharmacy, instead of the grocery store carrying it.

It was a wild hope, almost wilder than the idea that I, Grant Calhoun, could have found someone as incredible as Roxanna Reid to complete my life's formula.

"Hey, Pete." I probably looked crazed as I entered at this late hour. "Total longshot, but have you got any local honey?" Maybe I shouldn't be splashing to the world even an atom of information that I'd been looking for this particular ingredient. "My mom said she had seen it here."

"If you're looking for filtered, no. That's at the grocery store. Instead, I have some in raw form next to the beeswax lip balm on aisle seven. Raw is best as a balm. It sells out all the time, so I hope there's some left. People love it. Say it has medicinal qualities. There's a lady who puts it on cuts to heal them fast, she says. I know it works. I tried it myself."

Medicinal was exactly what I was looking for!

"I told my wife stocking it was a waste of money, that no one in Wilder River would pay thirty-five bucks for a half-pint of honey."

"How many jars do you have?"

Half an hour later, I was back in my lab with all six jars of Pete's stash of Wilder River honey—and the best idea for the formula. The key ingredient.

Inspired by the essence of Roxanna.

My girlfriend.

Roxanna, who loved the science geek in me. Who loved reading Yardley Gregson. Who kissed like she'd been starved for only me all her life. Who loved her dad but loved integrity more. And who had the most beautiful hair I'd ever seen. If I could get a single River Tresses customer to enjoy hair like that? Ka-ching.

Plus, no wonder that teen had gone berserk over Roxanna's beauty, assumed she was a celebrity. Fangirl must have had x-ray vision to see beneath Roxanna's hat to that gorgeous head of hair that only enhanced all Roxanna's other beauties—gorgeous enough she could be famous if she weren't so fixated on becoming a college literature teacher.

Well, those chestnut locks would be even more beautiful after I had developed the formula for River Tresses that would be both healthy for the scalp, thanks to the medicinal qualities of the honey, and would make the hair healthy with the spring water's unique mineral content.

This formula was dedicated to Roxanna Reid, the woman I just might love.

Chapter 17

Roxanna

I'd kissed Grant. A thousand kisses. And another thousand on Saturday, and another thousand on Sunday. We'd get tired of it someday, right?

Hardly.

Monday, as soon as shooting wrapped for the day, I hopped into a taxi and met him wherever he asked—this time, he took me to the library. I expected us to watch another BBC production, this time an episode of Father Brown, since we'd been so busy kissing and working we could only read the book for Twelve Slays of Christmas once each.

Instead, he had a surprise for me.

"I found a copy of *Royal Wedding*."

My heart skipped. "With Fred Astaire? The movie where he dances on the ceiling?"

"Well, the room spins, but movie magic makes it look that way. There's a bonus feature of how they made it at the end of the film."

I threw my arms around him. "Grant!" This was the best, sweetest thing! "Fred Astaire is my inspiration. He always arrived on set prepared—over-prepared—a total professional. I want to be just like him."

"It's one of your strengths. One of many." Grant gazed down at me with admiration that I could feel all the way to my toes.

He seemed really happy to be with me. Maybe even as happy as I was to be with him.

The next week's book was Miss Marple, and we reserved the library viewing room again. Public displays of affection were becoming our thing—but only public if someone happened to glance through the glass of the door.

We pulled the blinds.

The following week, we read Hercule Poirot.

We spent Thanksgiving apart—which about killed me. I went back to Reedsville to see some cousins. Grant spent it with the Calhoun cacophony. I missed him like I missed oxygen. I delivered a payment to that toad, Thorn Atkins. Some holiday break.

But then I returned to the clear skies of Wilder River the following Monday.

While at work, Domingo couldn't get enough of me. I was all giggles and smiles. He said I was the living essence of the flurries inside a snow globe—a joy to film.

"Thanks," I said, with an apology in my heart, since I couldn't focus, couldn't even eat. I could barely breathe until it was time to meet Grant—for book club, for dinners, for laughing and talking and movies at the library and kisses.

After book club, during the Kinsey Milhone week, we stayed and talked until Freya closed up. We talked in his truck until my sleep alarm demanded I leave him, but that felt like surgery.

The following night, we met again, work tired, but energized in each other's presence.

"I have a surprise for you." He sipped a strawberry milkshake through a straw, even though it was only ten degrees outside, and snow piled the sides of the streets on that late-November night. "You're going to like it."

"I am?" I took a small sip of my chocolate shake, but the chill of it made my stomach quake. "What is it? Or is it a secret?"

"Here's a hint." He set down his drink and turned toward me. "I'm making something in my lab. I'm going to dedicate it to you."

"Does it have honey in it?" I knew it did, since he'd said so when the idea hit him so hard that night after we'd first kissed near the Peppermint Drop Inn. It was the sweetest thing anyone had ever done for me. "I'm guessing it's a pharmaceutical." To be honest, I didn't know where he worked. The name *Wilder River Lab Company* didn't give me enough of a clue. I didn't pry. That was our deal. He could see my hair, and I could see his lab, but we didn't ask about each other's specific jobs.

"No other hints." He smiled and then we finished up our meal and headed to the ski lodge, where we took the elevator to the landing to see the night sky.

So romantic. Freezing, too. He wrapped himself around me in a back hug that made me forget it was winter and feel like I sat in front of a roaring fireplace on Christmas morning, sipping hot chocolate from the Hot Chocolate Shop. Warm, glowing, alive, but sleepy and happy and in love.

Hard core in love.

"Do you ever watch TV?" he asked.

"Only if I have time, and nothing taxing to the brain," I admitted sheepishly. "School and work take a lot out of me, so I have a soft spot for the Game Show Network."

"Do you play games?"

"Only crosswords, and only on plane rides—to keep my mind off the fact I'm in a hurtling hunk of metal in the sky."

"My mom would love to hear that."

"Does she have a flying phobia too?"

"She's possibly never been on a plane. She just loves crosswords—and Game Show Network."

"She sounds fun."

He talked about his mom some more—about her knitting habit, and about her mobility problems since his dad died. "She wields a mean knitting needle when she's upset. Like it's her Harry Potter wand, and you'd better watch out."

"I think I'd like her."

"She'd definitely like you. You should meet her sometime."

I froze. I was already pushing it by spending so much time with a local. "Sometime, yes." *After I'm done being Sanna for Gloss.* Why did that idea sadden me all of a sudden? I wanted to go back to school, right?

"Tell me more about your family," he said.

So, I told him about Grandma Reid. "I used to see my grandma more often." I didn't divulge the divide that I'd let come between me and her due to her devotion to Dad. For the first time, I wasn't as proud of my heel-digging resistance to Grandma Reid and to Dad.

"Family needs to stay close," he said.

"Some families should, yeah." Not mine. I'd never have a close family. I'd come to accept that fact. I'd have to have friends instead.

"So, speaking of phobias. You seem to like the book club novels more these days." He wrapped his arms around me, giving me a back hug as we gazed out over the valley in the silver moonlight. "Are the story themes bothering you less?"

"I guess they are." Yes, the *justice will be served* thing still grated on my already raw feelings, but they were getting more used to the idea, and it didn't sting like a thousand scorpions anymore. In fact, the better I knew Grant, the more realistic it sounded. The more possible.

Thank you, Grant.

The next day, I finished work, but Grant had a meeting. I was dying to tell someone about him—and my agent Bitsy wouldn't approve. I already knew that from earlier conversations.

Sooner or later, Danica and Jeremy would find out. Especially if things progressed between Grant and me on the course they seemed to be barreling down. *What's the destination here?*

It felt like … marriage.

***

The next morning, after filming and while Grant was at the Wilder

River Lab Co., I texted Danica. *Can I come down to your gymnastics studio? Hang out? Chat?*

If you want to chat about Grant, I'm all ears. Come on down. I have soup in a crock pot.

Soup sounded amazing. Except when my tummy was too fluttery with thoughts of Grant, I had been eating a lot more lately. Food felt like an old friend. And Domingo hadn't said anything negative, nor had Bitsy. I must be twitterpating away the calories.

"So it's official? You're dating?" Danica's eyes bugged out. We sipped the creamy potato bacon soup in the Christmas-bedecked break room of her gymnastics shop. "I had thought he was under a deadline at work and didn't have time to date."

Interesting. He'd never said anything about a deadline. But then again, we didn't talk shop.

"My work is pretty intense, too, but we make time." Our time together was intense as well, what precious little there was of it. "He asked me to his family's Christmas party."

"As I predicted—he's everybody's type. Even yours. And you're apparently his—also as I predicted." She sighed too heavily for the moment.

"What is it?" I asked, my hackles shooting up. I'd heard warning-sighs before.

"It's just that—never mind." She shook her head. "He's great. I'm really happy for you both. Opposites sometimes attract."

"We're not as different as you might guess. We both love literature and our families. He might be more science-brained than I am, but I can talk the sci-fi talk. It bridges that gap nicely."

"Yeah?" Danica stirred the hot chocolate with the tiny straw, her brow still furrowing. "What did Grant say about your undying crush on Captain Vartigan?"

"He commented that Vartigan is a complex character—not initially likable based on charisma, but based on his well-honed skills, and that we can't necessarily base our opinions of someone in real life on our initial interactions with them. Sometimes a lot goes on beneath the surface."

Danica's head snapped upward. "Speaking of below the surface, Roxanna, has he told you about his work?"

"Some." I'd been to his lab, but something told me I shouldn't mention that fact. Non-employees likely weren't allowed in there. "I haven't mentioned my work to him, thanks to my contract prohibiting it."

"I know you're trying to lie low." Danica grimaced. "What I don't get is why Gloss is making you film here in Wilder River."

"Because it's beautiful here?" My answer rang hollow. Bitsy had brought up a similar concern, and I'd forgotten about it until this moment. "It's not forever, but I can't complain, since it fits with my goal of attending the book club." And seeing Grant, day in and day out. I might even want to come back. After.

But I can't forget about finishing school. Or quit my job.

"And your goal of hanging out with Jeremy's cousin." Danica gave me one of those smiles that told me she felt a little sorry for me. "Look, Grant is great. But like your favorite sci-fi star, he's complex."

I almost fired back a retort that I knew about his complexity and was falling in love with it, but I hadn't told Grant that yet.

Danica continued, "Won't you let me set you up on a date with someone else in town? I happened to meet a local medical professional, someone doing his residency at the local hospital."

What? No! Cody Haught? Definitely not. "Dr. Haught is in the book club with us."

"So you know how incredibly attractive he is, with all that swagger and the amazing hair? Plus, he's a *surgeon.* A highly competent one. Everything from C-sections to organ transplants. He's a high-value target, if ever there was one. Don't miss your chance."

Why was she doing this? I thought she had been the one to push me toward Grant in the first place.

"Cody Haught is amazing, agreed. But I can't, Danica." Dr.

Haught wasn't for me. Or, more like, I wasn't for him. "We knew each other a little in college, where I learned there's someone already taking up all the space in his heart. Besides, I'm seeing Grant." So much so I couldn't ever picture *seeing* anyone else.

"Fine. But don't put all your hopes in the Grant holiday hamper." She put her soup cup down.

"I'm not." That wouldn't have been a lie a couple of weeks ago, but today, it sat squarely in the Fib Zone. "Fine, I like spending time with him."

"His whole world is tied up in his job and the company he works for, Roxanna."

Whom did he work for? Under normal circumstances, anyone would've known this by now, a month or more into a relationship. But, since my contract restricted discussion of my job at Gloss, asking him where he worked would've opened the topic and I would've sounded lame saying I couldn't tell him back. "All I know is he's a chemist."

"He's a chemist, all right. At River Tresses."

"The beauty products company?" I pushed my chair back a little, the leg catching between the seams of two tumbling mats, and making me half topple. "They're Gloss's rival."

But we had gone to Wilder River Lab Company, not to River Tresses.

It could be the laboratory arm of the River Tresses' parent company. I could've smacked myself in the forehead. That made sense for a town this size. There couldn't be two major laboratories for full-time chemists.

Danica pulled a tight smile. "River Tresses is also one of this city's biggest employers, coming only after the seasonal jobs at the ski resort."

Steady work, year-round.

Oh. Wow.

That meant, my company was Grant's company's biggest competition. *I* was the embodiment of Gloss, literally their poster girl.

He'd seen my hair. He'd heard someone call me "Sanna."

Danica's right. I shouldn't put all my eggs in the Grant basket. He was going to hate me when he found out I was his—and his town's, and his grandfather's legacy's, and his dream's—mortal enemy.

I needed to tell him.

Before his family's Christmas party Wednesday evening, as soon as work ended.

Unfortunately, work demands gave no opportunities to meet up before then, and I didn't think it was the type of thing we should discuss over text.

Heaven help me.

Heaven, help us.

Chapter 18

Grant

"**M**om, this is Roxanna."

"*The* Roxanna?" Mom worked her way out of her recliner and took Roxanna by both hands. "You're even prettier than my Grant said. But he also said you have beautiful hair. Why wad it up in that eyesore of a hat, dear? It's a wasted opportunity."

Roxanna squeezed my hand so hard it might fall off.

Oh, right. I wasn't supposed to tell anyone that Roxanna had hair. Er, whatever. After she whipped it out at the lab, she explained that the "weird situation" where she had to keep her hair hidden was due to a silly challenge at her freelance job. But she didn't have much longer to go and wanted to keep hiding it.

"Mom." I steered her to better topics. "You and Roxanna have something in common. She likes watching reruns of old game shows."

"You do?" Mom lit up like the Christmas tree in the corner of the house. I let the two of them chat for a while about Bob Barker.

Roxanna bantered like a skilled master, charming Mom like a genie, granting Mom's wish for a fellow-fan.

"Do you prefer Richard Dawson or Wink Martindale? Be honest." Mom sounded deadly serious. "And don't let the fact I have a signed photo of Wink on my nightstand sway you."

"Wink all day long." Roxanna waved the air. "I watched old episodes of *Tic Tac Dough* every night after work to wind down and fall asleep when I was in high school."

"Oh, I'm so glad you agree." Mom was in heaven. "Though, Richard does have his fine points." She named a few, and Roxanna added some points about Pat Sajak. His hair, mostly.

I went for plates of food for both of them at the buffet, where the line stretched from Mom's kitchen off into the screened-in porch family room. Cold, but with the heating lamps, still warm enough for a dozen aunts and uncles and cousins to congregate, laugh, and talk over the Christmas music while they ate.

There was a jar of honey next to some homemade wheat bread— one of Mom's many additions to the buffet table. I lifted it and sniffed. Yes—the same floral notes as the Wilder River honey Zed had sourced for us secretly from the farmer. We now had enough of a supply to get us through ramping up production.

Everything was working out.

Roxanna was my lucky charm.

Danica, Jeremy's very pregnant wife, popped out of her chair and came over to me. "I see you brought Roxanna."

Right. Danica knew Roxanna as an old friend. That made our connection even better—a shared history, interlinking family and friends. It felt more and more right every day.

"I assume she told you we're dating."

Danica pulled a tight smile and placed a hand on her belly. Did she not approve? "I'm so happy." She didn't look happy. Maybe she was having a contraction. Better not, since we'd have to call Cody Haught after hours.

Not a festive thought.

"Is there something you're not telling me?"

Now her tight smile turned fake. "No, nothing. I'm happy that she gets to experience *this* family. She told you about hers, right?"

I gave her a grim nod. "It sounds like she's been through a lot."

"Don't put her through more, Grant." Danica's eyes implored me. "Tread carefully?"

What did she think I was? A heartbreaker? "Of course. I care about her." So much.

Someone called to Danica. "Your husband needs attention, Danica, or he says he's going to perform a motorcycle stunt near the ice sculpture."

Danica bolted as fast as a heavily pregnant woman could, and I turned to pick up two plates off the stack.

Too slow.

"Grant!" Vance, my great-uncle, came over and patted my back. "We saw that girl you walked in with. Bad hat, right?"

"Terrible," I agreed. "But in spite of the hat, she's great. Her name's Roxanna. We're officially dating." I might as well announce it to everyone listening—and they all were. Extended family *always* got overly invested in my social life. "Dasher likes her."

A little roar of approval rose and fell.

"Get her under the mistletoe soon, eh?" Uncle Vance elbowed me. Luckily, the buffet cleared, and I was able to fill the plates for Roxanna and Mom.

A minute later, I delivered the plates lined with pinwheel cookies, candy cane divinity, and marshmallow corn flake wreaths—Mom's favorite—dyed green and with the little red-hot candies on the top to represent holly berries. "You okay with a coma-inducing-level of sugar?"

"Love it." Roxanna took the plate, though she didn't taste anything. No wonder she stayed slim. She barely ever ate anything I gave her. "Thanks."

"I hope you two didn't decide to go off on a road trip to Hollywood and camp out on Chuck Woolery's doorstep."

"Actually, your mom was just telling me about the time she fell off the roof of the house and broke both her elbows."

Oh, that story. "It was bad."

129

"She said you pretty much handled everything for her for a year."

"Not everything." Close, though. "She's lucky I was in Wilder River since I'd just taken the job at the plant."

All the blood drained from Roxanna's face, and the plate wobbled in her hand.

"Are you all right? Excuse us, Mom. Roxanna should sit down." I took her plate and steered her toward a quiet corner on the other side of the Christmas tree and settled her on a couch. "Can I bring you some water?"

Roxanna shook her head, but she pressed her hand to her chest. Something was definitely wrong. "It'll be all right." She looked up at me, her eyes liquid, swimming with concern. "Won't it?"

"Won't what be all right?" But it didn't matter what *it* was. If we were together, nothing else could go wrong. "It will, Roxanna." I wrapped her in my arms. "My mom obviously loves you. The rest of the family will as soon as they know you. Just like"—the words choked me up for a moment. But I forced them out. "Just like I do."

She bit her lower lip, her gaze darting back and forth between my eyes, as if searching for sincerity or deceit.

"I mean it." I pulled her closer. "Yes, it's fast, but when it's right, I guess it can be fast."

"Grant?" She placed her hand softly against my cheek. "I don't want any of this to end."

Did it have to? Maybe not. Maybe I could finish up the product formula in my lab, and then I could focus on some ideal plan for convincing Roxanna Reid to become a permanent part of my life's formula. That would be the best reward I could imagine for my hard work. Even better than saving the factory and the jobs and Wilder River's economy for my great-grandpa.

I'm so in love with her.

Then, I had an idea. I would make tonight really cool for her. It'd be step one in my *convince Roxanna I'm good enough for her* plan.

Chapter 19

Roxanna

He loved me!

And I was such a coward.

We sat side by side on a floral-patterned velvet sofa while all the Calhoun family continued their holiday party. There was a talent show, where the younger kids performed songs and dances, a short play of the Nativity, and now a visit from Santa.

"You seem to be feeling better." Grant pressed his nose to my ear and kissed a spot just below it. "I'm so glad."

"I've never been to a family Christmas party like this. It's so great." I was completely at home—despite the scary truth that still needed to be talked about. The family activities had distracted me for a minute —better than crossword puzzles on a plane.

After Grant embraced me behind the Christmas tree, my doubts and fears had turned to trust and hope. He'd said he loved me!

It was like all my misgivings and terror had been touched by a magic wand. Those three magic words of love had wielded the power to change my very being.

I was so in love with him—and it felt like falling from a cliff. But maybe onto a soft landing. Into Grant's strong, protective arms.

Had he been honest when he'd sworn none of the barriers between us mattered? The sincerity had been so alive, palpable. He'd more or less made me believe that even if I was Sanna, he could love me. That we could work all things out. That nothing could stand between us and our love.

We were so right for each other!

All the little kids were lining up to get a chance to tell Santa their wishes. But mine had already come true.

I even loved his mom. It was like we'd been friends for ages. We bonded over game shows at first, but it turned out we both loved vintage recipes that required obscure ingredients, that we'd both been on vacation to Calgary, Canada—her driving and me flying—and we'd loved the same stores in the Mall of the America *and* attended the Stampede.

Most of all, we both loved Grant.

That was the biggest bond of all between us.

Weird, I'd confessed to her before I even confessed to Grant.

Well, as soon as we were alone again, he wouldn't be far behind.

Santa left, and another activity began. Wow, this family was full of Christmas traditions. Could I love it more? Probably not.

"Time to open Christmas crackers!" One of the younger cousins brought us each a little wrapped box in shiny cellophane paper, each with a protruding fuse of twine. "You pull it and it explodes. There's a toy inside—and a fortune for the new year."

"Can I have the blue one?" I asked, reaching for one of them.

"No!" Grant grabbed the blue one first, leaving me with the red one. "Sorry, I love blue."

That was weird, but I took the red one.

"On the count of three." Grant counted, and we pulled the strings.

Pop! Out came a spray of confetti, candy, a folded piece of green paper, and a plastic ring with a huge candy gem on it. "Santa went all out." I unfolded the note.

At the top, it said, *Grant has an announcement to make.*

The little cousin grinned at me. "He's got an announcement to make." Her grin widened, and she turned around and with a surprisingly loud voice cut through all the conversations and commanded everyone's attention. "All right. It's time for Grant's announcement."

Grant stood up, cleared his throat, and said, "Merry Christmas season, everyone. I want to announce that, in case you hadn't heard, Roxanna Reid is my girlfriend." He paused for cheering and then started up again. "Get to know her, please, because she's probably the coolest person on the planet. I'm the luckiest guy in Wilder River, and in the whole world that she lets me call her mine."

The room went dead silent. Was it a good silence or a bad one? I couldn't tell, but Grant didn't seem to notice. He pulled me to my feet and kissed me.

A smattering of clapping began, and then the little Christmas cracker delivery-girl hugged our legs. The applause grew. I loved this family. I felt more accepted by them in an hour or two than I'd felt with my own family in decades.

Please let me be a part of this somehow. If only. ...

"Let's go?" Grant took me by both hands, collected our coats, and we went out to his truck. "I know you have early work hours. You said so. And I want to respect that."

"That's nice."

"But it's also a little selfish. While I was kissing you in front of everyone, I had another breakthrough."

"You did? What kind?"

"Just about the thing I'm working on in the lab. Do you know?" He took my hand and laced his fingers through mine. "Whenever I kiss you, I feel like I'm being infused with pure light. It's knowledge and power and strength. I'm so much better when I'm with you, Roxanna. I love you."

The words sprinkled over me like a shower of goodness. "I—I think I love you too, Grant."

He pulled up at the ski lodge. "I don't want to let you go. I want to go with you."

"You'd better go." I wanted him to come with me, too. But we

133

weren't ready for that. At least I wasn't. Not with the heavy secret I was shouldering. *I have to tell him the truth.*

He leaned across the bench seat and kissed me. "I'm heading to the lab and finishing my project tonight, thanks to the breakthrough I had earlier, thanks to your kiss. But when my project is finished, I'm going to start asking for a lot more time with you."

My work filming in Wilder River was winding down, or so Bitsy had hinted earlier today. Would I be back in Wilder River to spend that time he requested?

I'd make that happen. Without him, my soul was parched. "I think I can do that."

"Don't just *think* you can." He kissed me, came around to let me out, and waved as he drove away.

Upstairs in my hotel room, I peeled off my hat, swung out my hair and twirled in a circle, letting it free in the centripetal force. When I stopped, it wrapped around me like a hug from Grant. This, this was the happiness I'd always wanted. Could I grasp the proverbial brass ring? Was it mine?

Speaking of rings.

From my bag, I pulled the little candy ring from the Christmas cracker. Had he placed it in there, or was it one of those happy accidents? Didn't matter. I unwrapped it, slipped it onto the ring finger of my left hand, and held it out and admired it.

Not only did I love him, but Grant had become the first man who not only believed in me but had taught me to trust again. I hugged myself and fell onto the bed, curling into a happy ball and counting the minutes until I could see him again.

Escaping by doing the equivalent of a mental crossword puzzle to forget the fact I was lying to him about who I really was.

Chapter 20

Grant

"Bingo!" I poured in the last CCs of spring water, and the reaction began slowly, then increased, and then settled into a beautiful swirling mixture.

"You got it?" Lucy stood at my side.

I jumped. "Where did you come from?"

"It's eight in the morning. How long have you been here?" She frowned. "Not all night again."

"The deadline. But I got it! It's finished." I poured out the cooled formula onto a square glass plate, and Lucy examined it in all the ways Lucy always did.

Was I right? Had the product finally coalesced into success? I watched her intently.

Lucy looked up. "I think you're right. This seems to be it." A smile erupted across her face, showing her front twisted tooth. "Good work, Grant. Maybe it wasn't so bad that you left your position as a desk warrior upstairs after all, and they won't have to cut all our benefits, and we can all live happily ever after. Like a fairy tale."

That was one of the nicest things any River Tresses employee had said to me since my career shift. "Thanks." I handed her the printout of my finalized formula. "Keep this on lockdown."

"Right." She anxiously read it, grinned, and then folded it in half.

"Well done, Grant."

Zed walked in. He scanned the room. "Wow, messy for this early in the morning." Truly, the bottles and powders and oils—and the honey containers—were scattered everywhere. "I hope a mess means you have good news for me. Because"—he looked grim—"they moved up the deadline again. They say they need it *today,* Grant. No more delays, and they mean it. Gloss is breathing down our necks, and—hey, why aren't you giving me one of your stern rebukes about not rushing science?"

I released my suppressed grin. "We got it, man."

Zed crossed the distance between us in three strides and threw his arms around me. "That's great!"

He never hugged. "Why so emotional?" I asked.

"Oh, nothing. I'm just happy for River Tresses." He coughed a little, as if clearing away even more emotion.

Unexpected, but maybe my enthusiasm for keeping the town's biggest industry alive had infected others in the company. "Let's celebrate—but not today. I need to collapse. Didn't sleep all night."

"No, let's go report."

Good idea. "Sure."

I took off my lab coat and grabbed my winter one so I could take off as soon as we finished upstairs. Zed and I rode the elevator to the floor with the suits' offices. Mr. Bolton, current director of the River Tresses plant, was there with other board members, smiling but stressed as always in his signature rust-brown suit.

"I'm happy to report some positive news." I gave them the results and Lucy's stamp of approval, and they agreed to run final tests as soon as possible—but it sounded like they trusted me, even without every single testing requirement.

"We'll fast-track this, since we know you would never do anything to jeopardize River Tresses, Grant." Mr. Bolton shook my hand with hearty vigor. "Good work getting it done in time to roll it out at the first of the year. We need this win. Otherwise, we'd have to cave to the pressure to let Gloss go through with the hostile takeover."

What! I dropped his hand. "Are you being serious?" Hostile takeover! Wasn't that only in my imagination? Why would they even want our company? We were not a threat. We were just healthy competition.

Mr. Barton gave me a few details, and they weren't pretty. Not only would they be buying out the River Tresses product line, they'd assume ownership of the plant—which they could shut at will. "Can you see why we rushed you?"

"I can. And you could've told me."

"Management-privilege restrictions. Sorry, Grant."

I got it. I'd been on their level. I missed being in the know, and yet I couldn't help thinking I'd done the right thing exiting when I had.

Barton congratulated me again, and I exhaled all the way down in the elevator and didn't stop buzzing all the way home in my truck.

Just as I'd cleaned up and adjusted the pillow beneath my head, my phone chimed with a text. I grabbed at it like an eager cookie thief. "Please be from Roxanna."

Nope.

Ivory. *I get it, Grant. Really. Your rejection based on the fact you're dating Roxanna Reid. But do you really have to choose someone who's the literal face of Gloss? Don't you worry she will betray you?*

What was that supposed to mean? I nearly texted back to demand an explanation. But then, I remembered—this was Ivory. Classic Ivory move, anything to sow seeds of contention and doubt just to get a reaction. I did what I should've done a long time ago and blocked her from my phone.

Then, I closed my eyes and fell into a sleep full of dreams of kissing Roxanna Reid.

When I woke up, there were three texts waiting. One was from Freya, of all people.

Can you come down to the Hot Chocolate Shop a little early? I need a favor.

Sure, I could do that. I owed her a lot.

The next two were from Roxanna. Roxanna! I went all giddy like I was fifteen or something and my teenage crush had noticed me at a school dance.

Hey, Grant. Good morning.

Seeing those words gave me a vision of what it'd be like to hear them from her lips in person someday. Maybe every day. And soon. Now that the formula was submitted and on its way to approval, I was actually free.

Free!

I moved to the next text from her. *Sorry. I'm going to miss the book club meeting tonight. Something came up.*

My airplane of happiness crash-landed. How could she not be there? When I had such good news to deliver—and not by text? This announcement was good enough it needed to be in person, so that I could thank her in person for the inspiration she'd given me, and tell her the formula was dedicated to her. Let her try it out, even.

Maybe I could even express my thanks and devotion to her with a different kind of ring than the candy one from the cracker last night.

An hour later, I braved the newly fallen snow and headed to the Hot Chocolate Shop.

"You're here." Freya held out a box labeled Christmas lights. "Jeremy Houston told me you've been the chief hanger of Christmas lights at your mom's house for the past decade or more."

"Jeremy is a traitor of the highest order." I smiled and took the box. "You have the hooks up already?"

"I'm not a cruel tyrant." Freya directed me back outside, where two ladders leaned against the north side of the building. "Thanks. My husband has to take tickets at the basketball game at the high school, or I'd rope him into this. I just thought maybe you'd want to talk."

Oh, right. The woman had been a psychiatrist in her pre-chocolate life. "About what?"

"Oh, there's a thing called cognitive dissonance."

"I've heard of it." The struggle when a person's belief and a newfound belief were in conflict, and the person had to either adjust behavior or thinking patterns. "You think I'm going through it?" What could make her think that? The only thing I thought about today, other than the joy of having saved River Tresses and Wilder River's economy, was Roxanna.

Roxanna, Roxanna, Roxanna. My future with Roxanna. Her playing snowball-catch with Dasher. Buying a house near the Peppermint Drop Inn and raising our babies with their second-cousins, Jeremy and Danica's kids. We'd have to get started right away, since Danica was almost ready to give birth to their first, and—

"Aren't you?" Freya asked, interrupting me. "Experiencing cognitive dissonance on some level?"

"Why would I be?" But in a rush, Ivory's text slammed back at me. "Is this about Roxanna?"

"Not about her personally. She seems perfectly great."

"She is." Emphasis on perfect. For me. "It's crazy fast, but I'm probably going to propose to her. Don't tell anyone, though. You're the first to know."

"I'm honored." Freya didn't say any more, but after we'd strung three more strands, it started bugging me.

"So, why should I be concerned about Roxanna? Is there something I don't know?" Since Roxanna had been open about her dad's struggles, about her own financial trials, it seemed she'd shared with me the deepest things of her soul. In fact, "She showed me her hair, Freya. Took off the stupid hat. I honestly don't think she's hiding anything from me."

"If she showed you your hair, then, well—" Freya moved her ladder and didn't expound.

"What? Is there something about her hair?" Ivory couldn't be right. "She doesn't actually work for Gloss. Ivory started that rumor." Ivory was the Grand Duchess of Rumors in Wilder River. No one around here believed a single thing she said anymore.

Freya set down the half-empty box of lights and planted her feet in the new-fallen snow. "Come with me."

She led me inside the shop and pulled a stack of mail out of a drawer and set it on the counter. From inside, she pulled a flier. At the top was Gloss's glossy logo. "Does this face look familiar?"

I turned it around to see the model right-side up.

All the energy drained from me, from my scalp to toes, flowing out the soles of my feet. It was Roxanna. I stepped back an inch, but the base of the photo had a calligraphy scrawl with the words, "I only use Gloss products." And it was signed, "Sanna."

"I hope this doesn't make any difference to you or your feelings. That you've dealt, like you said, with the cognitive dissonance. Or that you never felt it in the first place."

"It's—" My mouth went so dry my tongue filled my throat. Sand followed. And a few pebbles. Then a boulder.

Finally, I managed to speak again. "It's fine. She's absolutely the best person I've ever known." My reply sounded weak, even to me.

"Good." Freya broke into an approving smile and took the flier back. "Your character is impressive, Grant. Not a lot of guys as devoted to their careers and their hometowns could be as magnanimous and forgiving as you are. You're impressive. No wonder every woman in town would give anything for you to date them or their daughters." She patted my arm. "Hey, I've got an appointment right now. Can we take a rain check on finishing hanging the lights?"

Seemed the light-hanging hadn't been the actual reason for the meet-up.

"Sure." I still couldn't breathe. "And I might not be able to make it to the book club tonight."

"Did you read the Rex Stout novel?" Freya lifted a sharp brow. "If not, you know the consequences."

"I do. And I read all about Nero Wolfe, obese armchair detective from Montenegro. Or is he?" Had I convinced Freya of my innocence? "Anyway, Stout is great. I read it and loved it, but I just have something important to do."

"Sure." She smiled again. "When my two top book clubbers both have to be gone on the same night, I get it. The legend of the Hot Cocoa Shop as a matchmaking agency lives on." She winked.

It pierced like a poison dart.

Why hadn't Roxanna told me she worked for Gloss? Or, especially, that she was their most famous hair model? All the clues of her deception stacked up like a confiscated weapons dump on the planet Chylock.

Roxanna and I needed to have a serious sit-down discussion. Now.

I drove toward the Wilder River Ski Lodge. Would they let me up to her room? Well, they'd have to.

As the elevator took me to her floor, I hummed loudly to push back my doubts.

My own transgressions slammed me, as well. For instance, I'd taken Gloss's top model *inside* the most secure laboratory of River Tresses. Lovesick fool!

Well, at least I hadn't divulged any industry secrets to her.

Argh! Except the honey! And the Wilder River spring water! Those comprised two of the most top-secret industry secrets of the moment. What if Gloss asked her about them? Would her contract and loyalty to her employer obligate her to tell?

My head pounded. I'd either fallen in love with the best girl in the world or my life's biggest enemy. I was here at the hotel to find out.

I lifted my hand and rapped on the door of the lodge's biggest suite—because where else would Gloss's top model be staying?

141

Chapter 21

Roxanna

A harsh knock sounded at the door, and I tightened my robe around me. There wasn't much time before my contract negotiations. It came again, almost angrily. I cracked open the door.

"Grant?" Why was he here? I rubbed the towel through my wet hair, glad it wasn't still dripping and soaking through the back of my bathrobe. "What's going on? You've never come up before. Is it because you couldn't wait to see me any longer? And you wanted to …" My lame attempt at innuendo hung in the air, and I expected his signature eye-twinkle to appear.

It did not appear.

"Can we talk?" His voice was grave.

Did I have time for a grave talk? Not really, but this was Grant. He wouldn't be here if it weren't vital.

"I just finished work, and I have an interview for contract renewal with my bosses. Can we meet after? Although, these could take some time."

"It'd be better now."

"Okay." I let him in, but his footsteps were more like stomps.

Uh-oh.

"Nice view." He sank into a chair by the window and glanced out at the ski slope—which was teeming with night skiers under the lights after yesterday's heavy snowfall.

"You okay, Grant?"

"Contract renewal. You work for Gloss."

"I do." He'd figured it out. "I—I thought you knew. There was that girl who called me Sanna. You work in the hair care industry. I'm pretty well-known."

Of course, all that hadn't meant Grant himself had recognized me. *It was on me to come clean to him. To confess the truth.* "You heard it from someone else."

"Yeah, not from you."

I sank onto the ottoman in front of his chair. "Grant. I am not allowed contractually to talk about my work."

"You had me sign a contract declaring me your Location Adviser. You showed me your hair."

Yeah, that had been a huge risk. And probably a technical breach of contract. I'd risked a lot for him. If only he understood how much I trusted him!

"That contract you wrote and we both signed? It had a special place of honor on my nightstand."

"Had? Past tense?" I stiffened, and the air grew thick between us. "What's going on, Grant? I swear, I would have told you if I'd been legally authorized to do so."

"I thought we were being completely honest with each other."

"We were. We are." My breath sped. "Why didn't you know?" He could've looked me up online.

"I didn't know, Roxanna. Or Sanna. Or whoever you are."

"But, that girl at the Christmas Hamper event. But, Ivory—" Surely, he'd seen how Ivory reacted to me and that should have stirred his curiosity. Ivory probably surreptitiously told him, knowing her and women like her, and—and he wouldn't have listened to her. In fact, I'd *told* him to never listen to her again. "I'm so sorry, Grant."

He chewed his knuckle, looking out the window at the snow on the slopes. Then, he looked back at me, his eyes meeting mine. "You're not hiding anything else, are you?"

"I wasn't *hiding* the fact of my employment from you. I was honoring a contract. I wasn't allowed to talk about it, Grant. You would've been the first person I confided in." But, would he have been? I wasn't sure. "Well, Danica knew. She was the only one. But she knew from before. It was Gordon Gloss's personal decision—as to when I came to shoot in Wilder River. The bigwigs made me sign away my life, basically." Had he forgotten how much I needed this job? Or why I needed it?

I hadn't been as direct with him about Thorn Atkins as perhaps I could've been. Oh, heaven above! Help me! Help us!

Grant scrubbed a hand down his cheek. "I want to believe you. I want to trust you, Roxanna."

"You should. You can." Desperation bubbled up in me. Was I losing him? Over something as fleeting as this? My phone alarm sounded, telling me I had to leave. "I'm so sorry, Grant. I have an unbreakable appointment." If I skipped it, I would lose the final sum I needed to pay off my debt to Thorn Atkins. "Can we continue this later? Please?"

He shifted his weight, giving me a stare hard enough to crush diamonds.

Why was he still hesitating? Was my employment such a big stumbling block for him? Sure, we worked for opposing companies in the same industry. Sure, Gloss was bigger, and I was a key player in their marketing. Sure, that could be a thorn in his side—*if* River Tresses didn't have a great product line and customer base of their own.

Gloss was giant, but not everyone loved products from giant companies. There were lots of types of customers. River Tresses had its own.

"Fine. Later." Grant left without a backward glance.

I threw on some clothes and raced to my appointment, but sitting at that table, I could barely concentrate, and Bitsy kept nudging me under the table. Once, she even stomped on my foot to keep me from jiggling my leg.

"We're really happy to renew with you." The negotiator had a grin as wide as the Joker's, and with even worse lipstick. "We appreciate your professionalism. Our time in Wilder River has been extremely productive."

I couldn't answer. I was crumbling inside.

Bitsy picked up the dropped ball. "Sanna is the consummate professional. She comes to work prepared and focused. You'll be able to count on her for years to come." Another shove beneath the table.

"Oh. Uh-huh." So much for professionalism. But how could I respond to these back-and-forth volleys that meant nothing to me if I lost Grant? While everything in my gut said I was losing him?

Chapter 22

Grant

A full week passed in a daze. I couldn't think, create, or do anything but read books.

They didn't help.

Without Roxanna, or my trust in humanity, everything was bleak.

Under a gloomy snow cloud, I returned to the Hot Chocolate Shop. The book club was just starting, but I took my mug of steaming cocoa and sat near the front window. Freya shot me a concerned look, like she knew exactly what had happened, but she had a book club to run.

She made a sign to join them.

I didn't join.

Even though I'd read and enjoyed *Fer-de-Lance,* book one in the series by Stout, I couldn't bring myself to squeeze conversation out of my crushing trachea.

After it ended, I'd hash things out with Freya—I owed it to her, since she'd been the one to finally open my eyes.

At the window, I stirred the beverage into oblivion, until a guy with a toupee and a too-bright tie came over. "Y'all from around here?"

His y'all sounded fake.

"I'm a Wilder River native. True blue, through and through." My standard answer. I didn't add the Richard Grant Wilder connection part, though I could have. This tourist seemed like he'd appreciate it. "You enjoy your stay skiing or whatever." I dismissed him.

He did not catch on to my dismissal. Instead, he pulled out the other chair at my bistro table and sat down. "It's pretty here."

"Yeah."

"But the prettiest thing is the women. One in particular."

Oh, great. Was this one of Ivory's crazed fans? They sleuthed her out from time to time, since she was the most world-famous resident of the town. "I wish you the best, buddy." But Ivory wasn't going to be swayed by his choice of wardrobe or haircut. Those things mattered far too much to her.

"Thanks. Then, with that wish for luck, maybe you can tell me where to find her."

"Probably not."

"You haven't even heard who I'm looking for."

I didn't respond.

"You know a Sanna?"

My stirring stick froze in mid-stir. "The hair model?"

"The very one. I heard she got a major payout, and"—he lowered his voice—"she owes me. Big time. I'm supposed to have Christmas vacation paid for with my wifey and kids already. But she's in arrears. Ten years in arrears, more like. I want to get my share before she pilfers it away on fancy cars or a house or something."

Good grief! What kind of payments was Roxanna supposedly negotiating from Gloss in her contract meeting? Cars? House? But, she said—

Slowly, I began stirring again. "Wish I could help you, but I'm not your guy."

And maybe I wasn't Roxanna's guy, either, if she interacted with sleazy characters like that, and if they hunted her down in mountain resort towns. Just how much of her life was she hiding from me?

Finally, he realized he couldn't pump me for any additional information and left.

"I thought I'd find you here." Mr. Bolton sat down hard, the lapels

147

of his rust-brown suit flapping on impact. "Lucy said you have a standing appointment here every Thursday night for a book club."

"Mr. Bolton?" What was the plant manager of River Tresses doing, seeking me out after hours? "How can I help you? Is there"—I probably gulped—"bad news about my formula?" It should've come back from accelerated testing this afternoon. "I swear, it's the best hair care product we can give the world."

"Yeah, that's just it. *We* aren't going to be giving it to the world after all."

"What does that mean?" My blood congealed. "Who is?"

"Gloss."

No, they weren't. "I'm not following you."

"Stop lying to me. It's not a joke."

"Me?" A thousand chills ran through me. "Why would I lie?" In all my life, I couldn't ever remember being accused of lying.

"But you are. You did what I *never* dreamed you'd do."

"I'd never lie to you, Mr. Bolton. You should be as aware as anyone that I'm the most devoted employee at River Tresses." Had he any idea what kind of salary cut I'd taken to try to rejuvenate sales? Or any idea how much pressure I navigated from inside myself every single day, just to try to keep the whole town afloat? "I need you to be clear, especially if you're accusing me of misconduct."

"Someone on the inside tipped off Gloss to the secret ingredients." He lowered his voice. "Both of them."

But—but! "That's not possible."

"Then how do you explain this?" Mr. Bolton opened his phone and showed me a photograph. "Read that."

It was an ad for Gloss—the one I'd seen earlier on Freya's counter, the one with Roxanna's huge brown eyes begging me to love her. The one with her signature across the bottom.

Then, I saw the real seal of doom. On a large gold-foil-like sticker image were the words, "New and Improved—exclusive Panukaa oil formula PLUS miraculous natural honey and spring water!"

A primal groan rose from my gut, but died on the way out of my throat.

Gloss had cornered the market on the Panukaa oil, making Zed unable to get any for River Tresses. And now Gloss was using local spring water and honey? I died inside.

It was all thanks to Roxanna's leak! Or was it my own fault? I was such a dupe!

I had taken her to my lab. The ingredients were all around us, and I'd mentioned them specifically to her, thinking a graduate student in English lit would have zero interest in chemicals of any kind.

I hadn't banked on her being a corporate spy. What did they call it? A honey trap?

I'd been totally honey trapped. And she'd even smelled and tasted like honey.

I hung my head, placing it in my hands, right there in front of Mr. Bolton. "I was the consummate stooge."

"So this means my suspicion was correct. *You sold us out.*"

Roxanna had sold me out. All of me—my job, my business, my history, my dreams. I couldn't look at Mr. Bolton, but I told him that I'd been deceived, and that I'd broken protocols by allowing her into the laboratory.

"You can fire me on the spot. In fact, you should. I didn't tell Gloss, but it's all my fault."

"It'll kill the town's image of you. Of your whole family."

I didn't care. "I deserve it." It'd kill the town. I'd killed the town.

"Okay, then, Grant. Much as I hate to do it, you're fired."

He patted my shoulder and then walked out the door, holding it open for someone coming in.

It was Roxanna, who strode toward the seating area. "Huzzah! It's my ninth time at book club! Three more and I can finally go see my professor and get my thesis proposal looked at. When I do, I'm buying Hot Hawaiian Ham Sliders for everyone."

My stomach soured—even more than it had a second ago when I'd been unceremoniously fired. *Because of her.*

The harder you love, the sharper the dagger when they stab you in the back. Gandalf was back.

Well, the Grey Wizard and his so-called wisdom needed to take a hike. I hung back in my seat next to the coat rack. What could she possibly be doing here, and why would she show her face after what she'd done?

"I'm so happy to see you all." She was taking off her gloves and heading toward where the club members sat around the fire. She kept blathering on, twisting the knife. "I didn't think I'd be able to make it, since I had a mandatory meeting with my bosses. But it turned out amazing, and—sorry, Freya. I'll save the chatter. Did I miss the whole discussion?"

Freya shook her head with warning and pointed in my direction.

Roxanna turned, and our eyes met. Her hair was down and flowing over her shoulders. She looked like a goddess. Or a hair model. Or the most beautiful woman I'd ever seen.

Just looking at her tore me to shreds.

"Hi, Grant." Her elation of a second ago dropped like a lead balloon. "I thought you weren't going to be here tonight." She came over beside the table where I sat, and glanced nervously over her shoulder at the crowd, whose eyes were all trained on us.

"Same here. I thought you were in contract negotiations." I couldn't care less who heard me.

The book club discussion had quit for the moment. All of them stared at us—from Quentin to the Whitmores. Even that surgeon I used to envy. Let them all hear what she'd done to me. To all of us.

"About those negotiations ..." She broke into a blinding smile. "I was glad they renewed my contract, but I never expected the huge bonus they offered me, but it's going to change everything! I'm free!"

Yes, it would change everything—for everyone. I bit back the bitterness, but some seeped through in my tone.

"Bonus?" I asked, acid in my tone. It had obviously been a payoff for information. Not modeling. "How much?" In other words, *how much was my town worth? How much was my family's legacy worth?*

"I—I'm not sure this is the place to say." She glanced back at the group, who were all still riveted on us. "Grant, please. You look so angry. But the news is so good! I need to go see that lawyer."

"Lawyer? You'll need one." My voice was barely more than a croak. "After what you did to me, to my company, to the people of this town, you deserve to be in prison."

"What? What are you talking about, Grant?"

"Forget it, Roxanna. I can't believe I let myself care for you. You're as shallow as Ivory. In fact, you're no better than your criminal father."

Chapter 23

Roxanna

I stood in the middle of the Hot Cocoa Shop, broken to pieces, like an empty cocoa mug thrown to the floor.

Grant couldn't have wounded me more deeply if he'd used Captain Vartigan's space sword forged in the fires of the volcano on the Glypsim planet. I teetered, my shoulder knocking against the coat rack and tipping it over. It whacked against the front window frame, knocking down some beribboned evergreen garland.

"Can you two discuss that outside?" Freya asked. "We're trying to conduct a book club."

"Come on, Freya. This is far better than Nero Wolfe," Quentin complained. "Such an old slob."

But Grant took my elbow and led me out onto the front porch of the Hot Chocolate Shop. The night air crackled with cold, and the breeze blew like a crying baby through the needles of the pine tree out front.

"Grant?" My voice was strangled. "What's going on? Why are you accusing me of a crime?"

"You told Gloss about the ingredients in my formula." He stabbed his finger at a picture of me on his phone screen. A Gloss ad. I hadn't even seen that one yet, but I caught a glimpse of the logo.

Sickness sloshed in my gut. "No, Grant."

"Then how do you explain the payoff money? The *bonus*."

"That *wasn't* payoff money." Then again, the Gloss execs hadn't explained why they'd been so generous, other than to say they wanted to keep me on board. My knee wobbled, and so did my voice. "Please, Grant. I didn't. I wouldn't. Ever."

"I can't believe I trusted you. You're cut from the same cloth as Ivory. Out to destroy everyone in your path to fame and success." Grant stamped past me down the wooden steps, leaving me alone with a slam of the truck door. Dasher barked at me from the truck bed.

Even the dog had turned hostile toward me.

What had I done? If only I knew!

Everyone in the Twelve Slays of Christmas book club piled out the door and stood on the porch. Their mouths hung slack, and they stared openly at me. I reached for my head, but my usual hat was gone. They'd never seen me with my hair down, and—

"Sanna?" Ellery Whitmore said, aghast. "You're *Sanna*?" Her voice soured. "Your company is trying to ruin Wilder River. I heard Gloss is attempting to take over River Tresses. After that, they intend to shut down the whole plant."

What? Really? "I—no, Ellery. I didn't know any of that."

She smirked as if she didn't believe me either.

Quentin turned on me, too. "Do you know how many Wilder River residents work for River Tresses? Four thousand. That's one in five residents. And one of them is Grant. Who'd be crazy if he ever spoke to you again."

He wouldn't work there for long. Grant would obviously be fired for fraternizing with the enemy—me. No wonder he thought I'd told. We'd been close. I'd heard him mention some ingredients in the formula, whether I'd realized it at the time or not.

"We trusted you, Roxanna." Freya frowned. "Mr. Bolton was in here earlier, firing Grant. Now the news chatter online is saying River Tresses plant is actually shutting down production—right before Christmas." Her eyes narrowed. "Did you cause that? Did you betray all of us?"

"No!" I hadn't done it. I hadn't done anything, had I? All I did was star in a commercial for the competitor. *On the home turf of River Tresses.* Bitsy had been sounding the warning bells about it ever since the assignment came.

"Were you attending this book club to try to pump us for inside information?" Bing Whitmore folded his arms across his chest.

"Are you okay, Roxanna?" Cody Haught winced—at least he cared, believed in me, somewhat. "I've known you a long time. Are you being misrepresented?"

"Yes! Totally! Well, not totally." I'd been forced to keep information from everyone—I'd lied about being Sanna—when this town wouldn't have accepted me as my stage name. My head spun. "I'm so sorry."

"What's the truth?" Even Cody's gaze hardened. "The truth, Roxanna."

The truth. Right. Finally, I spoke. "I wasn't pumping anyone for information, I swear."

Just because Grant had unintentionally passed me information—which I hadn't even mentally processed at the time—he found it easy to blame me. Likely, everyone would. But I hadn't funneled it to Gloss, or to anyone else.

"I was just modeling. It was a *job.* A temporary one, necessary so I could make enough money to pay Mr. Atkins and go to school at the same time, and get out from under that fiend's thumb." Ouch, my head hurt. Just mentioning Thorn Atkins's name caused a jackhammer to go off in my brain.

"I think you'd better clear off." Freya shooed me down the steps into the swirling snow.

The temperature had to have dropped below freezing, but I barely felt it. Nothing else mattered right now if Grant didn't believe in me.

If that was the case, how could I believe in him? I'd trusted him with my deepest secret, and he'd stomped on it. Jumped to conclusions, called me a criminal!

Worst of all, he'd equated me with Dad.

I could barely walk, but I headed out in a blizzard and wandered around Wilder River, the tears streaming and potentially freezing to my cheeks.

A minivan pulled up beside me. "Roxanna? Is that you?" Danica had rolled down the passenger side window. "Get in here."

I couldn't. "No one should touch me with a ten-foot pole, Danica." I kept trudging. "You'll be tainted."

"Stop that." Danica hustled around the van and steered me into the passenger side. "Let's go. Don't talk now."

Bless her for not asking about why my hair was down—or anything else. Especially for not asking immediately whether Grant Calhoun was the source of the tears. For not letting me walk in the frigid weather.

She drove us to her nearby gymnastics studio, the Candy Cane Cottage, and brought me a plate of dinner—that Jeremy had made, thank goodness. Danica wasn't the best cook. It took a minute for the after-quakes of my earlier sobbing to subside, but eventually, I was able to eat and then think. At last, I gave her the whole story.

Spilling my guts left me crying with my head down on Danica's break-room table, sobbing and sniffling.

"The whole thing is really unfortunate," Danica said, squeezing my shoulder.

"It's way more than *unfortunate!*" It was downright tragic! My voice was muffled as I protested into the laminate tabletop again, for the umpteenth time. "I never told Gloss about those ingredients! I swear it. When I fell for him, I didn't even know Grant worked for a rival company. Until you told me, I thought he was a standard chemist somewhere at a generic laboratory. I had no idea."

"I could tell this was on a whole new level." Danica patted my back and then rubbed a soothing circle. "You told me you didn't even cry after that awful day in court."

True. I'd been so stoic, watching them take Dad away after sentencing. "I really thought I loved him, Danica."

"You might still love him."

That was the problem. I couldn't turn off love like a spigot.

Danica hugged me. "You have handled so many awful things before in your life."

This was different, though. This wasn't about someone else's actions. This was about my own. "I lied to him."

"You abided by a contract. That's honesty, even if it doesn't feel like it."

We went the rounds about this for about ten minutes. Finally, I could breathe a little again, based on Danica's reassurances.

Even though I was beyond crushed, I couldn't stay flat to the ground. I had to do something about my life—even if I couldn't do anything about Grant and his opinion of me. Even if I could never have him as part of my life again. "Could you help me with two things, Danica?"

"Of course. What do you have in mind?"

"One involves a *lot* of gold tinfoil, and the other involves driving me somewhere that I don't think I could drive myself home from."

Gravely, Danica nodded. She knew exactly where I needed that ride.

Chapter 24

Grant

"Selling!" I staggered internally, but gripped the wall of Mr. Bolton's office. There was nowhere to grip, though. Smooth wood paneling. I was slipping away, literally and figuratively.

I shouldn't have come here. I wasn't welcome. It didn't matter. What mattered was what I had to say to Bolton, to everyone on the board.

"What do you mean, we're selling?" Selling *out* was more like it. And more like something I should be getting used to by now.

"We don't have a choice." Mr. Bolton set his mouth. His rust-brown suit was rumpled after such a horrible day. "And since you no longer work here, it's not clear why you care."

I cared because—because I *cared*—whether they wanted me on staff or not. And I had shares in the company—literal shares, not just a history with the company or the town. A lot of literal, corporate shares. What incentive would I have to tank the business?

Argh!

"It's also not clear why you're here. Do I need to call security, Grant? Have things devolved to that point? Please, at least maintain your last shred of dignity. If you're hauled out by one of our officers, someone will see. And then everyone will know. Wilder River is a small town."

Bolton wasn't wrong. I hadn't planned on coming back to River Tresses to plead my case to Mr. Bolton, but my conscience demanded

157

that I at least tell him the whole truth, and maybe with the full information, the executives could make better decisions about my firing, and about everything related to this sham deal.

"Please, Mr. Bolton. River Tresses can't sell out to Gloss." They were rolling over and dying. "We have to stand up to them. David and Goliath, you know?"

"Considering your contribution to the disaster, I shouldn't be entertaining you or giving you this information, but"—he heaved a rumbling sigh—"because of your heritage in this town as a Wilder, I respect you enough to tell you that selling is our only option." Bolton stood looking out the window of the corner office at the ski slope. "They have us beat on every front, thanks to your corporate-secrets betrayal."

I wouldn't argue that fact right now. I needed more information from him, not a verbal fight.

"If I'd still been in management and not downstairs, I wouldn't have entertained the idea of selling out for a split-second. What will happen to the factory? To the jobs?" To Wilder River, and to Richard Grant Wilder's legacy?

"That will remain to be seen. When they're full owners of River Tresses, their board will make those decisions."

I tugged at my hair hard enough I could've almost torn it all out from the roots. Just like this day was tearing me from my roots in Wilder River, separating me from home, family, history.

Love.

"There's got to be some way to solve this without selling." But how?

Zed would know. He cared about River Tresses as much as I did. Almost as much as he cared about his family.

"Where's Zed? Can you get him up here?"

"He's at the hospital with his son Dallin."

That's right. The surgery had been scheduled for right before Christmas. How could I have forgotten? I should've been there for him.

A sick thought hit me. What would Zed do without medical insurance from the company? Dallin's health care costs were astronomical.

Downstairs in my truck, an audiobook launched through the stereo when I started the engine, a dramatized version of Charles Dickens's *A Christmas Carol*. "Mankind was my business!" the voice of Jacob Marley shouted. "The comprehensive—" I shut it off.

I drove straight to the hospital. Inside, I ran into Dr. Cody Haught. My skin crawled reflexively, but he was probably the only person who could help me.

"Did you perform the surgery for Dallin Windsor?" Transplant surgery? That was big, for a local doctor. Usually those critical cases got sent out.

"I did."

"Wow."

"It was successful, but I can't tell you more than that."

Praise be! "Are his parents here? Zed is my childhood friend."

"They're all in recovery. Tell the nurses I said it was all right." He patted my back. "You're not half bad, Calhoun. I didn't like you at first, but you're all right—as long as you're not too harsh on Roxanna Reid. She's a whole lot of all right. Probably more all right than you."

Dislike resurged. What did Cody Haught truly know about Roxanna Reid, the traitor of my life, anyway?

Recovering my equanimity, I found Zed and his wife in the recovery room beside Dallin, who was still sleeping and connected to more tubes than a subway system.

"Zed," I said softly, giving him a bro-hug. "How's Dallin?"

"Doing well. Dr. Haught did amazing work on the transplant, and we didn't even have to travel to Reedsville. That was better for Dallin, and Pamela, and all the rest of my kids."

"He came extremely highly recommended," Pamela said. "I wish we could keep his skills here in Wilder River, but I hear he's going to Mendon."

I tried for a sad face, but I was probably a weird smiling sad face.

159

"Yeah," Zed went on, "it'd be nice if he could do the follow-up surgery for Dallin in six months."

"Follow-up surgery?" But—but without River Tresses being in business, Zed wouldn't have a job, which meant the family wouldn't have health insurance. Insuring a dependent with a *lot* of preexisting conditions could be horrible. Why did Zed seem so unworried?

In the past, he'd been totally preoccupied by that. Even his hee-haw had suffered at times.

"I'm so happy for you all." I gave him our usual back-slap of friendship and hugged Pamela, who went home to be with her other kids.

"Thanks for coming by." Zed rested a hand on my shoulder. "I'm sorry we won't be working together anymore. I guess all Camelots must come to an end, eh? Do you like my literary reference? Good job developing the formula, by the way. I guess my advice to read a few books to preoccupy your conscience did help. Not to mention having that girlfriend inspire you. Gorgeous head of hair on her, eh?"

"Yeah." Was it just me, or was Zed acting glib about the demise of River Tresses? Maybe he was just overjoyed at the result of the surgery. That made sense. We talked for several more minutes, and then it was time to leave. "I'll catch you later."

"Okay." Zed dismissed me. "I'll see you around. Somewhere. Maybe we'll both work for Gloss if they reopen the plant. You could come back upstairs with me again. It'll be like old times."

An undeniable uneasiness sloshed through my stomach. Definitely glib. And as much as I hated myself for even thinking it, I turned around and uttered the least palatable words I could imagine.

"Zed, did Gloss hire you?" It came out like broken glass.

"What?" Zed's eyes bulged out. "Did someone tell you that? Did Roxanna Reid tell you? Your girlfriend is their biggest asset. That makes sense."

He was talking at guilt-speed. I'd known Zed long enough to see what was coming next. The faster he talked, the sooner he'd slip up and inadvertently admit his wrongdoing. I didn't interrupt, and he spluttered forth a million excuses one after another until the inevitable—

"I did what I had to do, and it worked out—all right, Grant? I don't have a perfect life like you. I'm not the town hero. I have to be my family's hero first and foremost, okay? Don't look at me like that."

"Did what you had to do? In other words, corporate espionage?"

"It's not corporate espionage. It's more of ... information sharing with a potential business partner."

As only a marketing exec, Zed didn't have the right to decide who was a potential business partner and who wasn't. "Do you realize what you've done?"

"It's going to be fine. Gloss *loves* the new River Tresses product formula you developed. They're already advertising it. Under their umbrella, of course. But chances are strong they'll produce it right here in our plant. You're worrying for nothing."

For nothing! I'd lost my job! I'd been accused of lying! He'd potentially tanked the whole economy of our town. Worst of all, "Zed, you shared the formula with them?"

"I could see the way things were trending. If you'd been upstairs, where you should've stayed all along, you would've seen it coming, too."

"But, whether you knew it or not, you let me falsely accuse Roxanna of telling Gloss about the Wilder River honey and local spring water."

She hadn't sold us out, but I'd full-on accused her of being a criminal—to her face, slashing her to pieces. Ruining whatever trust I'd built up in her.

She might never forgive me.

"Hey. Let's keep things straight. You're the one who jumped to that conclusion. I didn't even know you'd done that." He lifted a shoulder, and then he sobered. "Be real with me, Grant. If you were Dallin's dad, what would you have done?"

Good question. But I had an answer—a clear one, steered by the rudder of my ship of integrity. "I wouldn't have lied, Zed. I wouldn't have sold company secrets to our biggest rival. I wouldn't have done that to my best friend. Or to my family."

"What are you talking about? I was *helping* Dallin. Helping my family."

"You might think that, but I believe I know someone who would rather have *died* than have their dad sell his integrity for anything, even an organ transplant. You were shortsighted. When Dallin finds out, and he will, I just pray he can learn to forgive you someday—and himself."

"You don't know that! You don't know any of that!" Zed was shouting now. "You've never had a sick son on the verge of death. When that's been your lot in life, then you come to me and tell me about what all is entailed in integrity." He stormed out, leaving me at Dallin's bedside.

I gazed down at the sleeping boy. So frail, but with a chance now.

The horns of a dilemma impaled me: tell Mr. Bolton and the board about Zed and get him in trouble, or not. Ruin my best friend's life and career, destroy the faith of his family in him—all the week before Christmas.

Or, should I let River Tresses and all the employees go down in infamy and flames?

The machines monitoring Dallin beeped.

Roxanna Reid hadn't sold Gloss my formula or secret ingredients. She wasn't the criminal I'd accused her of being. Much as I hated to admit it, Cody Haught had been spot-on about her—she was a whole lot of all right, and a whole lot better than I deserved.

I'd been a jerk!

Was there any way to make things right? To show her how sorry I was, that I knew how wrong I'd been?

And besides that top priority, was there any way to make things right for everyone else?

Impossible, said Gandalf.

For once, I agreed with the cranky old wizard.

162

Chapter 25

Roxanna

Danica waited in the minivan while I climbed the concrete steps, grasping the railing like a lifeline.

Inside the several sets of doors, Christmas music—"Hark, The Herald Angels," of all songs—played like a non sequitur in the hallway of the prison, where I gave my name to the armed man at the front desk. Several minutes later, I was led inside.

My hands and knees trembled as I sat down across from him. He looked older. Tired. His beard's stubble was all gray, not even salt-and-pepper anymore.

For the first time in seven years, we saw one another face to face. Granted, a thick slab of plexiglass separated us, and we had to communicate through a pair of old-time telephone receivers, but we were together.

I don't know what I'd been expecting. Shaved head? A hundred tattoos? Missing teeth? Instead, he just looked like Dad.

That same Christmas music channel piped through the air in here, as well. The herald angels had wrapped up, and now came "Silent Night."

Well, I'd been silent too long. It was better to break the silence, for once.

"Hi, Dad." The sentence came out of me—actually emerged from my vocal cords. And it hadn't even felt like razor blades slicing my throat. "Hi," I repeated, since it had been possible and easy.

"Hey, sugar. How's school? You getting ready for Christmas?"

The words were so mundane. So normal. What had I been expecting? Immediate depth of conversation and apologies and closeness restored? Not sure. But not, *How's school? You getting ready for Christmas?* I exhaled. I could do this.

"I'm almost done with school. It took me a few years longer than I expected. I had to work a lot." Thanks to Dad's decimation of our finances. Ah, there was the emotion I'd been anticipating. All peppered with needles' points.

"Good for you! Working a job is good. I bet you've learned a lot of things by working your way through school."

I blinked a few times. "Yeah, actually." I'd learned a lot of things by working. Maybe as many as or more than I had learned in the classroom. But *life* things, not book things. Both were important, it turned out. Funny, I could see that all of a sudden. Maybe it was the "Silent Night" song's inspiration distilling on me. Music often had that effect.

"You know, I've heard a lot about your job." Dad described having seen me in a few magazines with Gloss ads. "Your grandma brought them in to show me. She keeps me updated." He told me about Grandma Reid's regular visits.

And I hadn't visited him once in all these years. I'd resented Grandma for visiting him, too. That was probably a mistake.

Why was my nose running all of a sudden? Why were my eyes prickling? I coughed that reaction away. "I'm here to ask you a question, Dad."

"Anything. I'm sure you're disappointed in me, but if I can ever win back your trust, I'll do anything."

Including telling me the truth? *Please, just don't lie to me anymore, Dad.*

"Why did you originally plead not-guilty?"

Dad leaned forward and placed his elbows on the windowsill, his head in his hand. "Oh, that."

Yeah, that! I could've screamed that he'd lied to me and to the court and to the world.

"I was a kid, Dad. At that age, I believed if you pleaded innocent, it meant you were. I defended you and your integrity to everyone. I *swore* to all who argued with me that you had done nothing wrong, that you must have been framed."

My voice was high-pitched, annoying, and I wasn't just on the verge of tears anymore. I was full-on fire-hose crying, eyes and nose and all. I wiped my face with my sweater's sleeve. "Dad, why? Why?" I hiccupped.

"Sugar." Dad's throat sounded constricted. It was grimy glass, but even I could see the tears streaming down his cheeks, collecting on his chin, and dripping into little pools on the chest of his orange jumpsuit. "You were so young, I thought you couldn't possibly understand that a not-guilty plea was a strategy, not a denial of guilt."

"I wasn't so young that it meant I was stupid." Other than being stupid and naïve enough to believe in him. "Why, Dad?" My throat was so tight it was like talking through a coffee straw. "I wanted you to be innocent. I needed you to be innocent."

He stared at his hands for a while, the phone cradling between his shoulder and ear. "I was just following the advice of my legal counsel." His features were as strained as his voice. "What would you have told me to do, Roxanna? Something different?"

"I would have told you to tell the truth."

Slowly, he nodded. "I've been reading a lot while I've been in here. You always liked to read."

"Okay." If he expected me to ask whether he'd read any good books lately, he'd be disappointed.

"The library has philosophers' books. There's the Bible. It does say not to bear false witness in there, you know."

Truly, *bear false witness* pointed pretty directly to lying in court.

"And, you did bear false witness? You broke a commandment? One of the big ten?"

"Yes. But it's more like *I* broke myself against it. What I mean is, the commandment didn't break—I did. And I'm paying my debt for what I did, but soon, that debt will be paid."

And did that mean he wasn't guilty anymore? I wasn't sure I could accept that.

You have to. The debt will be paid. In full. My conscience was so practical.

"From what I hear, you're paying my other debts." He frowned. "You didn't have to do that, Roxanna."

"How could I not? We owed them."

"I owed them, not you." He shook his head. "It's one thing to sell my house, but entirely another to sell Yeti. He was *your* dog, not mine."

But Dad had given me Yeti. That made Yeti Dad's.

Or did it? I wasn't sure.

Suddenly, I wasn't sure about a lot of things anymore. Had I owed Thorn Atkins? Me, personally?

"I wish you'd followed your conscience, Dad, instead of being led around by Thorn Atkins." The morally bankrupt lawyer.

"I wish I'd followed *your* morals, Roxanna. Not mine. I never would have been in here in the first place."

Well, at least he could admit that now. That admission, strangely, did more to soften me toward him than any other apology.

"I love you," he said, sighing heavily. "You've always been the best thing I've ever created, sugar. Like I said, I've been reading a lot, and I'm changing a lot. When I get out of here, I won't be the old me anymore. Grandma Reid can vouch for me. She was my biggest critic, but she has been the fastest to forgive from the minute she saw I'm really trying to change." He wrinkled his brow and dropped his hand. "That's a mom's job, of course. Not a daughter's."

Forgiveness was everybody's job. The Christmas song had changed again. Now, strains of "O Holy Night" wafted around us.

Truly, He taught us to love one another. His Law is love, and His gospel is peace. Love? Could I love Dad again? The thought did offer me some peace.

"I'll work on it, Dad. No guarantees how fast it will happen, but I promise I'll start to try."

"That's the best gift I could've asked for." He placed his palm up against the window. "Merry Christmas, sugar. You deserve so much better than you got. You deserve the best."

Outside, in Danica's minivan, I leaned my head against the seat as she drove us back toward Reedsville.

"You okay?" she asked after putting a few miles between us and the prison.

Was I? Hard to say, exactly. "I have the answer I went looking for—and a lot more to think about."

"Is that a good thing?"

Probably. "I think so."

"You said something about gold tinfoil?" Danica drove us through the freshly falling snow.

I told her about my plan.

***

"Well, if it isn't the supermodel who has taken *seven years* to pay her legal debts—and still hasn't given me the final payment." He smirked at me. "Sanna, is it? In the flesh."

"Merry Christmas, Mr. Atkins." I held up a heavy silver pitcher and pasted on my best Sanna smile. When I shook the pitcher, the clinking inside echoed through the whole Atkins and Atkins law office. "Silver and gold? You know the song from 'Rudolph the Red-Nosed Reindeer?'"

If he knew, he didn't say so. "What's this? Another one of your ploys to get me to accept your delays? Your father was ordered by the court to pay legal fees, and you chose to pay opposing counsel first. What kind of thanks is that for all the work I did to defend your father, Miss Reid?"

"This pitcher is filled with gold coins, like you asked to have me fill your dragon's lair. Remember?" I held it up with both hands, too high for him to peer inside and verify. "Why did you advise him to plead not guilty, Thorn?"

"That's lawyer-client privilege."

"Taking your advice is his biggest regret, Thorn." Other than committing the crime in the first place, I should've said. And losing my trust.

"Again, I can't discuss details of a case with anyone but the client himself." He lifted his nose. "What's in the pitcher?" His eyes registered dollar signs, gleaming with the gold-fever.

"Your final payment." I shook it again.

"Is that right?" His mouth spread in a greedy grin. "But you still owe me a lot of dollars, so this better be all of it. After I get back from Bikini-ville, I'm hitting some casinos."

I suppressed the eye-roll. Of *course* Thorn Atkins would spend the holy days in a casino.

I shook the pitcher again, and then slowly, I poured it onto his desk. "There you go. Enjoy your time in the casino." Coin after gold coin fell in a heap onto his desk, all golden and sparkling. "You like your silver and gold so much, unwrap those and count them." I dumped the final dollar coin from the pitcher and then chucked the container at the pile, making a few of them fall down.

"What's this?" He picked one up. "You can't pay *in-kind*. I'm not taking chocolate coins."

"They're legal tender. Dollar coins."

Thanks to Danica, Jeremy, and Bitsy—each coin was beautifully wrapped in gold foil. It'd only taken the four of us a few hours, during which we talked and listened to Christmas movies play on the nearby TV. It had been pretty fun, in fact.

Thanks, Danica. It was good to have one true friend.

"And there's more in there." I pointed to the wooden trunk I'd wheeled in on the hand-dolly but left in the corner. "All nine thousand four hundred sixty-three of them. Payment in full. Count them if you like."

He spluttered. "I have to unwrap all of them? You do know I don't have to accept this as payment."

"That's when the coins are pennies or nickels. No court has ruled against dollar coins." I'd done my research before putting my family through the multi-thousand coin-wrap party.

He growled but didn't respond.

"You'll have to have a money-unwrapping party if you want to spend it. Merry Christmas," I said. And good riddance.

I left that law office, finally free. My heels sprouted wings, and I flew out to Danica's minivan.

"We did it!" I beamed at her, leaning across the console and giving her cute pregnant self a hug.

"You did it, Roxanna. You earned every penny. At first, I was against it. It wasn't your debt to pay, but I saw your reasons, and you deserve to have that scumbag out of your family's life forever."

I did deserve that, didn't I?

So, why did the heel-wings suddenly shrivel up?

Two massive reasons.

One, I hadn't been able to complete all of the Twelve Slays of Christmas book club meetings so that I could finally induce Dr. Higgins to look at my master's thesis proposal.

And two, out there in the world somewhere near Wilder River, Grant Calhoun still considered me an unethical, money-grubbing, life-ruining villainess.

Nothing I could do about either of those things at this point. Wilder River hated me. And so did Grant. I might be able to forgive Dad—as a Christmas present to him and to myself. But Grant never would forgive me.

It was time for me to move on.

Chapter 26

Roxanna

A week went by. I spent it decorating my little apartment in Reedsville for Christmas and going gift shopping. Just a few days left until the holiday—and until Danica's baby's arrival. We planned the baby shower long-distance—Christmas themed, of course.

Finally, I resigned myself to the fact I'd have to find another book club. And I'd have to start fresh at zero-count attendances, according to Dr. Higgins.

No shortcuts for me.

In fact, no club on the list met again before the end of the year except, horror of horrors, the Russian literature book club.

Doom!

According to their social media page, *Crime and Punishment* was the upcoming book for discussion. How apropos. Oh, and look who was leading the discussion: *Henrietta Higgins*.

Double doom!

And yet, what choice was I left?

That night, late, I lay on my tattered love seat and turned the pages of Dostoyevsky by the glow of my little Christmas tree's lights. So far, it wasn't too bad, but it sure didn't hold a candle, escapism-wise, to Agatha Christie's books. Or any of the other Twelve Slays of Christmas selections.

My kingdom for a Miss Marple.

The next morning, Danica came down to Reedsville from Wilder River to finish up a little holiday shopping. She met me at the awesome bakery café, Bread & Breakfast, for brunch.

"If it makes you feel any better"—Danica sat across a plate of their famous German stollen bread from me with her mouth stuffed with almond slices and vanilla iced bread—"the guy who broke your heart is getting his comeuppance."

"Grant?" I hadn't spoken his name in over a week. I hadn't let myself even think of him. Well, not more than one million times an hour. "What do you mean, comeuppance?"

"Grant was fired for leaking information. Or from being tied to the leak. Not sure."

Great. That was on me, or so he'd said. Despite the fact that I hadn't done any leaking! Not that anyone would believe the truth. Whatever, all that ground was too well-trodden in my brain. Ruts worn deep.

"And," Danica went on, "Gloss is taking over River Tresses."

"No!" I dropped my Bread & Breakfast slice of sweet bread. "What is going on?"

"River Tresses can't compete, I guess. Jeremy was sitting in on the meeting since he's a part-owner in the company and had planned on helping River Tresses expand their plant into more corporate real estate space if they needed it with the new product rollout, and he told me about it."

Jeremy did corporate real estate, so that all computed. "What did he say happened?" My voice was thready, thin.

"Apparently, River Tresses had a huge, game-changing product in development, and the second they were about to release it, Gloss announced a new product formula with exactly the same ingredients."

"Oh."

"Gloss even had commercial footage for it all set to go—using the

171

videos they shot of you at the ski lodge."

The bread turned to ashes in my mouth. I really *had* been a key player in the demise of the town. "I'm—I'm so sorry, Danica."

"You had no idea you were being Gloss's pawn. They didn't loop you into the plan or anything. You were just making your standard salary—a good one, but standard contract."

Yeah, plus the bonus. Which they hadn't explained, even when I'd pressed. I had just assumed they'd been paying me hazard pay for having to travel to snowy remote areas for shooting this time.

How naïve of me! "What will happen to the plant? To the jobs?"

Danica shrugged. "No one knows. My guess is it might seem hunky dory at first, but Gloss will get tired of remote management. The River Tresses plant will ultimately have to fold. Jeremy's guess is it will take place in under a year."

"Fold!" And so fast?

"Six months is my bet." Her mouth formed a grim line.

"But what would that do to the Wilder River economy?"

"Not sure." Danica shrugged. "There will still be tourism, of course. But the year-round economy involves a lot of businesses, all dependent on people having year-round work."

"Businesses including your gymnastics studios."

Now I was going to cry again.

"Yeah, tourists don't sign up their kids for year-round gymnastics classes."

"Danica, Grant accused me of telling Gloss about the secret formula." I might as well own up to it.

"Come again?" Danica dropped her slice of pastry. "Told them what?"

"Well, I didn't sell any information, but I can see why he thought so. He'd told me the formula—well, two of its secret ingredients— when he thought of me as an English literature grad student and didn't know I was his rival's poster child." He'd even used those very words, *key ingredients*. Honestly, I'd let them float past my mind at the time, since I was so caught up in him personally, but it all made sense now, his reaction.

"You'd never do that."

"Not for any amount of money," I said. "Not after seeing what became of Dad's life."

"I believe you. Do you want me to talk to Jeremy? He can talk to Grant. He owes Grant, you know. Big time."

Did I want that? I wasn't sure. This should probably come from me directly, if anything happened at all between us. Maybe it was better to let sleeping dogs lie. Just walk away from the best thing that had ever happened to me.

"Grant's firing is too harsh," I said instead. "That wasn't a comeuppance, that was a life sentence." Selling the whole company—and tarnishing his grandfather's legacy of the town—was too much punishment for very little, if any, crime. It was just a hair care formula, not government secrets.

"Life can be so unfair." Danica heaved a sigh. "I do find it's sometimes unfair in our favor, though."

Not in this case. Justice was definitely *not* being served.

If only there were something I could do!

Danica let me off in front of my apartment, where a letter was waiting in my mailbox. Who sent handwritten mail these days? The return address was from Wilder River.

Dear Roxanna. A man's handwriting. I glanced at the bottom—it was from Grant. My eyes welled up, and I had to blink fifty times so the writing would stop blurring.

I wrongly accused you. I said horrible things. After what I did to you, I don't expect you to answer my calls, so I am going old-school. Maybe you'll read this and not just throw it in the fire.

I wouldn't throw it in the fire. Never. I clutched it to my chest, and then I pulled it away and read on.

My best friend from childhood is named Zed. He then explained that Zed had been the one to tell Gloss about the secret ingredient, and that he had a sick child and medical bills, which wasn't an excuse, but it was a reason.

I shouldn't blame Zed, since I haven't walked a mile in his shoes.

Then again, that fact didn't stop me from blaming you. And I had just found out how horrible it feels to be blamed for something I didn't do. I'm sorry I turned right around and did the same thing to you.

I should have trusted you. I shouldn't have said those things. Or even thought them. It kills me to know I must have hurt you.

Justice would be served if you never forgive me.

But I still wish you would.

Love—in spite of everything, Grant

I read and reread it a dozen times while standing in my kitchen with my leftover German stollen bread.

I crumbled my pastry to smithereens.

Oh, Grant! He knew I was innocent! But he was also fired. And his legacy was ruined, and maybe even so was the future of that great town where I'd fallen in love with the best man I'd ever known.

If only there were something I could do!

And then it occurred to me.

Maybe there *was* something I could do.

Chapter 27

Grant

"So, basically, I'm fired." I was sitting on Mom's old couch, the one where I'd hugged Roxanna, now only hugging one of Mom's old ratty throw pillows, a sorry substitute for that beautiful girl.

Mom wrapped gifts on a folding table in front of her recliner. "Pass me the paper with the Christmas trees on it, would you?" She hadn't reacted to my announcement yet. But she would. When she was ready.

I went on. "It's not the best Christmas news I could give you." I'd poured out the whole story to her, from Wilder River honey to Zed's betrayal. In fact, as I told it, it hit me that Zed may have been lying about the Panukaa oil. He could've been in cahoots with Gloss for months, and he must have negotiated the New Zealand farmer deal for *them,* not for River Tresses.

The javelin struck deep.

Mom reached for the scissors. "Well, to be honest, I'm really disappointed."

Nothing she said could've crushed me more. "I let you down." My head throbbed even more than it had the past two days while I'd mustered the courage to come over and give Mom the bad news. "I wish it could've been different. River Tresses means so much to our family."

"Oh, pish!" She wielded the roll of wrapping paper like a saber. "Not that!" She whacked the arm of the sofa. "My actual disappointment is you messing things up with that gorgeous girl Roxanna."

"Roxanna?" I knew Mom had liked her, but—

"You let her down."

No kidding. I'd sent her that handwritten letter, telling her how sorry I was, and that now I knew Zed had been the leak, and that she didn't deserve my criticism, and that Zed had an excuse, but that excuses weren't good enough reasons to make unethical decisions. And that I didn't expect her to accept my excuse, but to please forgive me anyway, even though I didn't deserve it.

Yet, I hadn't heard back from her, even though it had been a whole week.

"I more than let her down. I blamed her."

"That's stupid."

"You're right, Mom. Ding, ding, ding."

"You blew the sixty-four thousand-dollar question, if you ask me."

Million was more like it. "Don't remind me." I huffed out a breath, but the pain in my head and my heart remained. Pinching, pounding, emptying me.

"So, Grant. What are you going to do to make it right?"

"It's not like she could ever forgive me." I'd said unforgivable things that had cut right to her center—when I should have trusted her. Now, how could she possibly trust me? No, it was irredeemably broken.

"Of course she can."

"Mom, you don't know that."

"I do know, Grant. I know a lot." She picked up the scissors and aimed the pointy side at me. "When have you been one to give up? Remember your Hail Mary pass at the buzzer at the state championship football game? Anyone else might've given up. Not you."

Not ever, in that situation. I'd been trained for that. However,

"This is different."

"What about when you could see that Wilder River Lab Company needed a better product? You gave up your prestigious job, and that huge salary, and you went back to school as a returning student in a completely different field so you could save River Tresses. You totally didn't give up. You went way more than nine yards. You went the whole hundred yards."

"Again, different."

"Why? How so?"

"Because in those situations, everything depended on me. This has to do with someone else's autonomous feelings. It'd take a sheer Christmas miracle, and I'm not in charge of her feelings or in charge of miracles."

"Well, you know what I always say."

"What do you always say, Mom?" Mom had a lot of always-sayings.

"Where there's a question, there's an answer, and you just have to sleuth it out." She waved the scissors at the stack of novels on the table. "You're the one who keeps handing me the books you're finished reading. Why not be like one of the detectives in your new favorite books and *find the clues?* And then solve the mystery of how to get Roxanna's forgiveness. Where there's a will …"

Another one of her always sayings. I countered. "Where there's a will, there's a stronger opposing will and a stubborn resistance, Mom." Roxanna hadn't responded to my letter. Not even an acknowledgment text.

Even though my head rejected everything Mom was saying, my foolhardy, renegade heart still caught hold of the thrust of her words about the will and the way.

Maybe …

Mom cackled and clapped, her scissors clinking. "I can see your mind is already crackling." A grin broke out across her face, and she resembled her Wilder ancestors every time she smiled. "You need a

177

sidekick? All those detectives have sidekicks."

Not all of them, but some. And Mom wouldn't be my first choice of sidekicks most of the time since she spent so much time in that recliner. Then again, she was the one holding the weapon, and using the insistent voice.

"What are you thinking about this? Have you sleuthed out any clues already, Mom?"

"Cut to the heart of it." She picked up the scissors, opened and snapped them shut with a shink of metal against metal. "What is her greatest need, and can you give it to her?"

Sounded like Mom had been paying more attention to romances than to mysteries—even than to her game shows on TV.

"Not sure," I said. Wait a second— "Mom, you're a genius. She wants her professor to take a look at her master's thesis research proposal."

"And what's stopping that?"

Dun-dun-dun. "The book club attendance requirement."

"Well, there's your answer."

"Mom, you're a genius," I said again. I jumped up and hugged her, and then I grabbed my coat. "I'm going to the Hot Chocolate Shop."

"Bring me a Hot Hawaiian Ham Slider? Even though that Freya person dropped the *–pe* on the end of *Shoppe?* She does make a good sandwich. I can admit it."

"You got it. Anything!" I had one foot out the door already and was dialing Freya before I'd even started my old truck. Dasher barked once after jumping into his spot in the truck's bed.

It was as if he sensed action and was as ready as I was to go win back the girl we both loved.

As I drove—possibly too fast—it hit me: the honeysuckle scent of the girl I loved, combined with Mom's obsession with the healing properties of honey.

And I knew exactly what *else* I could do.

Chapter 28

Roxanna

Gordon Gloss droned on with facts and figures, occasionally pointing to his slide on the projector screen. I squirmed in my upholstered chair in the boardroom. Could this conference table be any bigger?

Didn't matter. This was my chance to make things right for Grant. Did he deserve it on every level after he'd been so cruel to me? No. But that didn't matter. Forgiveness was peace. Love was peace. I was going with the Christmas carol's lyrics—and hoping for a Christmas music miracle.

Anyway, it was like Grant's letter said: justice didn't always need to be served. Sometimes mercy should take precedence.

And maybe I can extend some to Dad as well.

I'd start smaller. With Grant.

"If you'll turn up the lights, Saunders," Gordon Gloss said, "I now cede the final two minutes of this meeting to a person we all know and appreciate, Roxanna Reid." When the lights came up, everyone looked around, as if scanning for a stranger. "Or, as she's better known to all of you, Sanna."

All eyes turned to me, and someone started some applause. I patted it out immediately and surged to my feet.

"Thank you for granting me some time to speak." It took every ounce of my Jessica Fletcher pluck to stand before the Gloss executives and make my case. As a shareholder, not just their company's face, I had a right to speak at the meeting, but that didn't mean I felt at ease.

Here goes. For Grant.

"Gloss has an image of integrity to uphold. The public trust is important." If only my knee weren't shaking as hard as it had during my first ever photo shoot. "If you purchase River Tresses based on scooping their formula, it will be based on industrial espionage."

Bitsy gasped beside me. "Roxanna!" she hissed, obviously shocked by the directness of my language.

"The shareholders need to know that at least one person on the board has made an unethical decision. One that affects the lifeblood of a community, as well as the very existence of a competitor."

From the far side of the conference table, Danica's husband Jeremy gaped at me, wide-eyed. The millionaire was a commercial real estate broker, and likely a major shareholder in Gloss, among other businesses.

But, next, his mouth closed, and he broke into an approving grin.

"Does the world deserve a breakthrough in hair health and skin care health? Yes. Should Gloss be the one to deliver it? Of course—if they're the ones who developed it. But not if they *stole* it." I didn't point fingers, but I glanced toward the newest face at this table, Zed, who was turning red. "Please make the right choices, everyone. Thank you."

I sat down. No one was clapping now.

The chairman looked up from his legal pad. "Those were strong words, Miss Reid."

"Only because I think the shareholders need to be aware of how their money is made. Some of us won't want dirty money, even if we make a tidy profit before the holidays."

"You're nothing but a model." Zed pushed back his chair and stood up. "I resent these accusations."

"No one accused you, Zed," Jeremy said, barely above his breath.

"She did!"

"Because they're true?" I said. How had he known I was leveling the accusations at him personally? It seemed he had a conscience. At least there was that. "You sold out your best friend. You and I both know that Grant Calhoun developed River Tresses' newest formula using the ingredients you revealed to at least one of the men here at this table."

Zed's forehead began to perspire. "I don't know what you're talking about. Board members, do you? Roxanna Reid is the traitor. She was the mole all along. Right? Right?"

The board didn't turn on me. They stood without a word and exited the room, going into private executive session, leaving me sitting there with Jeremy and some of the other shareholders.

Less than a minute later, they cracked the door and beckoned to Zed—as if with a skeleton's long, bony finger.

Zed now went white as a sheet and joined them.

At that point, no one dared speak. What would happen to me next? I could potentially lose my position, or Zed could.

One of our figurative heads would roll, that was for certain.

After twenty minutes, they returned—without the traitor.

Gordon Gloss leveled a look at me. "We're happy we just renewed your contract with us, Sanna. You've been a good team player."

Where was Zed? Had they axed him as soon as they saw him as a liability?

Oh, it looked like one of the vice presidents was missing, as well. A guy who'd only been with Gloss a few months. One I hadn't met personally, but whose leer had never sat right with me.

That answered that. Zed and his compadre in spying were gone.

"To thank you for helping us keep our corporate image untarnished, we'd like to renegotiate your contract for double the salary. Plus, we'll allow you to be a free agent, advertising for other products, as long as they don't compete directly with Gloss products. But we'd also encourage you to continue working with Domingo on filming and print ads. He's been insisting that expanding your brand will only help Gloss products. We happen to agree."

Wow. "That's very generous." I was floored! ! Expanding with Gloss *and* being a free agent? The world opened wide for me. *I might not need a fallback career. I might not need to battle Higgins!*

But I recalled myself.

"Well? What do you say, Miss Reid?" Gordon Gloss needed an answer. Now.

I had one—an answer he definitely wasn't expecting.

"Thank you very much, Mr. Gloss. However, to thank me, would you consider listening to my different idea? I think you'll see it as a win-win."

Chapter 29

Grant

I wasn't proud of the fact I'd sneaked into the Wilder River Lab Company with the big jar of locally sourced honey—and added it to the River Tresses shampoo.

"Bingo!" Lucy had said. "This is exactly it!" She lathered it up, smelled it, tested its antibacterial qualities, as well as the shine it created. "This is the winner. How did you come up with the idea of using local honey? Oh, right. Your mom's obsession with honey must have been the inspiration."

"Yeah." I couldn't tell her about Roxanna, but I also couldn't suppress the smile. "I chose Wilder River honey because it is almost all from wildflower pollen—fireweed, yarrow, Indian paintbrush, spirea. It's proven to have health benefits all over the world. The Apis polaris variety of honeybee is the northernmost living bee, and its product creates an insulating effect on hair during cold snaps. It's unique and we're keeping *this* ingredient a trade secret."

"Brilliant move, Grant. You didn't have to do it, you know, after what Bolton did to you."

"I know." But Wilder River jobs were at stake. And this could potentially save them. I refused to give up or give in. Grandpa Wilder's legacy still mattered to me, no matter what. "You'll take it to the board for me, Lucy? And don't tell anyone else?"

"Of course." Lucy then disappeared into the back room and returned with a plate of her famous baked goods. "You earned one." She offered me a pumpkin chocolate chip cookie. "Congratulations. Now, get out of here—before Kringle the security guard strolls past or Bolton shows up and calls security on you."

I shoved the whole cookie in my mouth and made a mad dash for the Hot Chocolate Shop. Oh! It was almost time for the next phase of my plan.

***

The cuckoo clock on the wall of the Hot Chocolate Shop sang twelve times. Noon. I'd sent Roxanna the text first thing this morning. Would she come back to Wilder River? She had to.

This just had to work.

It'd been four days since Freya had agreed to go along with my plan, and I was counting on everyone in the Twelve Slays of Christmas to come through for me. For Roxanna. For us.

"Hi." In bustled the Whitmores. They shrugged out of their coats and stomped the snow off their boots. "We did it."

"You read three books? A James Patterson, a Dashiell Hammet, and Lee Child in *four days?* All of them?"

Freya came in. "That's my brother for you." She handed Bing and Ellery each a cup of steaming chocolate. "If he says he's committed, he is."

Freya and Bing were siblings? I should've known that. The eyes were the same, now that she mentioned the relationship.

"I'll admit to fudging things." Ellery Whitmore sipped from her steaming mug. "It was a lot of time listening to three audiobooks at double speed while we worked in the stables, but they were good books. It wasn't a chore." She and Bing came over and sat down. "What was the big rush?"

In came Quentin from the jewelry shop. "Hallooo." He followed the same routine as the Whitmores—coat, boots, hot chocolate from Freya. "Good books. I love getting this bonus meeting for the holidays."

He found his favorite chair near the fire. "My wife would've loved it. She loved mysteries, especially mysteries with a stolen bride. Too bad we didn't get one of those in this batch. Maybe next year?"

"You want to do this mystery book club again? It wasn't too much of a chore?" I asked, joining them, glancing again at the clock. It was already five past the hour. Would Roxanna come? I'd been pretty insistent in my text. Maybe I should've talked to her directly, told her what was going on. "Where's Cody Haught?"

"Obstetrics. Delivery room." Bing jutted his chin. "Won't make it here today. I hear he's delivering your cousin's baby."

Jeremy and Danica's baby! Whoa. What a day.

I couldn't help being a little disappointed—in spite of myself, though. Cody Haught, for all his faults, had become a vital cog in the machine of the book club, including when he'd defended Roxanna while I accused her. I owed him a big apology, as well as a handshake of genuine friendship.

"But I heard from one of our customers who works at the hospital that he did read the books," Ellery said. "He wants you and Roxanna to work out."

Really? That made me choke up a little.

"So, do you all get why I cajoled you into reading three books in four days?"

"After your group text explaining how Roxanna was falsely accused, my wife would've come back from heaven and haunted me if I hadn't read them. You two deserve to be happy. Whatever we can do, we're all in."

Who would've guessed these fellow readers could turn into such a support system? "Thank you, everyone." I meant it from the bottom of my heart.

"Merry Christmas." Bing held up his copy of *Killing Floor*, the first Jack Reacher novel, as if in a toast. "And many more to come for you and Roxanna and Dasher."

"And any others you end up adding to the Calhoun clan." Ellery gave an exaggerated wink.

Wow. Just wow. The image of Roxanna throwing snowballs for Dasher to catch on Christmas morning flashed back into my mind. Only, this time, it was fuzzy instead of sparkling clear. Try as I might, it wouldn't resolve but stayed pixelated and blurry.

The picture will only come back into focus if Roxanna will come back and forgive you. Probably so, Gandalf, you cynic.

After a while, however, Bing and Ellery checked their watches. The cuckoo clock on the wall of the Hot Chocolate Shop above the holiday-decorated mantel struck the half hour.

I paced, looking out the window into the parking lot every few seconds.

Wasn't she coming?

She might not come. And after everyone had sacrificed so much! They'd have to leave, go take care of their businesses and families.

I agonized! "Can we wait just a couple more minutes?"

"She's here!" Freya pointed out the side window into the glow of the parking lot's lamppost. "What are you going to say to her? Do you need a minute alone? We could make ourselves scarce, if you want."

On one hand, I did want that, but—

"Hi." Roxanna's eyes were bright with excitement as she entered. She seemed only to see me. "How did you know I would need to meet with you today? Or that I'd be in Wilder River?" She took me by both hands. "Grant, I hope it's okay, but I need to talk to you before you say anything. I have some good news—and no, it's not about some bonus payout from Gloss, I promise. Actually, I also need a favor."

"Good news?" That was totally unexpected, but definitely welcome. Frankly, it'd been a while. "Sure. What's going on? What kind of favor?" And could it wait until after we'd met with all these people who'd given up their afternoons the week before Christmas to be here to discuss literature?

"I have a meeting set up with the Gloss execs in a couple of hours. If you can come with me."

"In Reedsville? Why would they want to see me?" They'd better not be offering me a job. I wouldn't take it.

"They're issuing a formal apology to River Tresses. And they're rescinding their purchase offer. And if I'm right, you'll be reinstated at the company—possibly as the vice president of research and development—if that's a position you'd like to take."

"What are you even talking about?" What exactly had Roxanna done for River Tresses? And for Wilder River? And for *me*?

"I can explain everything later, on our way to the meeting with the execs." She looked at her feet and then up at me. "If you're okay being with someone who hid the fact she was a model for your rival company."

"You couldn't hide your beauty, no matter what." I took her by both hands. "Remember when you said you'd read all three of the remaining books for the club on Freya's list? The ones by Lee Child, Dashiell Hammett, and James Patterson?"

"Sure. Why? What's going on?" She looked over my shoulder and seemed to notice everyone else gathered for the first time. "Why is our book club assembled? In the middle of the day? Grant?"

"Everyone else who has gathered here has read them, too. They read, and showed up, and are happy to do an accelerated book club marathon with you. Three meetings in one, for you to report to your professor."

Roxanna held the back of her hand over her mouth. "You all did that for me?"

"Grant did it for you, sweetie!" Quentin said, his white head of hair bobbing and his eyes crinkling behind his horn-rimmed glasses. "All we did was read books. Your boyfriend set this up and okayed it with your chump professor. By the end of our meeting, you'll be eligible to submit your research proposal, maybe even get it to the whole committee before they begin their Christmas vacations. You'll be ready to fire up your schoolwork and research come January first."

Roxanna turned and gazed up at me with wonder and amazement

dancing across her face. "You did this, Grant? After everything that happened?" Tears welled, but they didn't spill down her cheeks.

What did spill out was the truth, from my own lips: "I'd do anything for you, Roxanna."

"Oh, Grant! Grant Calhoun! I love you so much." She tilted her chin upward and kissed me. "You're a twelve on a ten scale. Or maybe a twelve hundred."

Everyone clapped. Then, we went over to the fireside and discussed the books we'd all read—but we talked at lightning speed, since Roxanna and I had an important appointment in Reedsville with the Gloss executive board.

***

Things played out just as Roxanna had promised. At the end of the meeting, Gordon Gloss extended a hand to me and we shook. "Congratulations! River Tresses told us they will be reinstating you as head of research and development. We can't apologize enough, but we hope this will begin to compensate for the damage inflicted on River Tresses."

It went a *long* way toward that.

I just felt horrible for Zed.

Somehow, someday, he would forgive me. I hoped.

***

Back in Wilder River again later that evening, I took Roxanna on a walk in the falling snow. She took my hand.

"Remember when we first took a walk in the snow?" she said.

"I remember." It'd been the night of our first kiss. I relived it in my dreams almost every night. Those memories had tortured me while we were apart, but now they could be a sweet dream again.

The sound of sleigh rails swished nearby, and Lenny hailed us. "Grant! Roxanna! Want a ride? I'm heading down by the river to give the horses a workout."

I looked over at Roxanna. "What do you think?"

"That would be very sweet. Memorable."

188

We climbed aboard, then spread the blanket over our laps.

The bells on the sides of the sleigh jingled as we raced down the trail alongside the Wilder River in the bright silver moonlight. Roxanna tucked herself up beside me under the fuzzy blanket.

"I'm happy, Roxanna."

"It was too long without you."

Only a few days had passed while we were apart, but it had seemed like an eternity. "Thank you for what you did for River Tresses. For Wilder River." I slipped my arm around her waist. "And for me."

She leaned her head against my shoulder, her hair spilling across my chest. "Thank *you*. I never would have dared ask the Twelve Slays of Christmas members to read extra books right before Christmas." She snuggled closer, and I felt complete. "Dr. Higgins might still come up with a way to say no, but—"

"Henrietta Higgins had better not say no, or she will have all of the Hot Chocolate Shop's most devoted book club members to contend with. And *we've* read a lot about murder."

"Murder is going a little far!" She laughed her trilling, soul-filling laugh. "It may be that I'd like a break from school. I might like pursuing some other dreams. You know?"

Lenny took us over a rise a little quickly, and my belly floated and fell. Roxanna took my hand, and our palms pulsed together as they touched.

"What kind of dreams?" *Do they involve me?*

"That depends. Can I ask you a nosy question?" she said.

"That's what all the detectives did in the books we just read. I'm braced for it."

"Good." She squeezed my hand. My heart flipped. "Maybe I'm jumping to conclusions."

"All our fictional detectives jumped to conclusions, but when they followed their gut, they were right every time," I said. My gut was hollering for me to say what I'd known for a long time. "Go ahead and ask." *So I can confess the truth!*

189

"Are you hoping what I'm hoping? That this could be a thing? That *we* can be a thing?"

I kissed her warmly and then pulled back to look into her beautiful eyes. "I don't need any more evidence to convict you of being perfect for me. I plead guilty of being in love with you, and I throw myself on the mercy of the court—will you marry me?"

"Absolutely. I love you, Grant. Case closed."

In the distance, the evening lights of Wilder River glowed in a steady pulsation, just like my inner light with each pass of Roxanna's light-filled kisses. Pure intelligence poured into me, knowledge of something greater that I could become than simply myself. That when combined with a woman like this—with *this* woman—the result of our melding of souls could be so much more than simply the sum of the parts.

"I'll be yours, Roxanna. Forever."

Chapter 30

Roxanna

Three years later

I leaned over the edge of the porch railing in the bright sunshine. Grant would be here soon, and even though the winter air chilled me, I couldn't wait inside for him. I wanted to catch the first glimpse of his truck heading down the long lane to our home.

"Okay, boy." I scrubbed Dasher behind his ears. I loved on him. "When is Mr. Calhoun coming home? I have to tell him something important."

Dasher barked once, and so I stepped down to the snow in the yard and scooped up a handful, which I molded into a snowball and tossed. Dasher ran for it, captured it in his jaw, and bit it into the powder. He barked and came back for more.

Just then, Grant pulled up in our circular drive, crunching packed snow as the tires blazed a trail in the newest blizzard's effects. A huge evergreen stuck out, loaded askew in the truck-bed.

"You said you wanted an epic Christmas tree. Here it is." He climbed out, hoisted it on his shoulder like the manliest lumberjack I'd ever seen. "Can you get the door for me, Dr. Calhoun?" He never tired of calling me that, since I'd fast-tracked my way through a PhD program at an online school, once I extracted myself from the clutches of Dr. Henrietta Higgins.

It'd been a ton of work, but totally worth it. Not that I'd be teaching English lit at a college anytime soon.

For lots of reasons.

I ran up the steps, and Dasher followed both of us, barking, into the house. A warm fire blazed in the hearth.

Grant found a good spot for it in the corner and leaned it against the wall. "I'll get it set up in a minute. Right now, I want to give you something—an anniversary gift." He reached into his coat pocket and pulled out a flat, wrapped package. "It's not original but I hope you like it."

I unwrapped the gift—obviously a book. "The newest Yardley Gregson!" I hugged it to my chest. "But how did you get this? It's not even Christmas yet." The book was set to launch in stores on Christmas Day.

"Open the front cover." Grant shoved his hands in his back pockets and rocked back and forth.

On the first page was a dedication:

To Roxanna, my friend and favorite doctoral degree recipient—and the star of my latest film.

I couldn't have chosen a better actress to cast as the Rygraff Princess in the first of the Vartigan Chronicles! I'm glad you're now Grant's Rygraff Queen.

Always, Yardley Gregson (but you can call me Cash)

I stared down at the words. "You got me an advance copy?"

"You're the princess in his hit movie. Of course you merit an early copy of his latest. Domingo got one, too." Domingo, the director, had loved shooting the snow-planet scenes—Rygraff being a snow-planet—right in Wilder River. Yardley had approved. They'd become fast friends.

In fact, I'd filmed volume one of the books, and I had a contract for the next three movies.

Didn't hurt the bank account—in fact, the movie deals had more than replenished every penny I'd funneled to Dad's attorneys, allowed me to buy back Mom's house in Reedsville (for when Dad finished serving time), and had freed up my tuition crunch and allowed me to transfer schools—away from Henrietta Higgins' tyranny—and had completed the master's degree in a single, extremely busy year. The best part was that since my movie deal included a percentage of the profits and the first one was a blockbuster hit, I was able to pay off what was left of young Dallin's medical bills. Something I felt I needed to do.

Of course, without Dr. Higgins, I might not have gotten to know Grant. So even the most irritating rock in my shoe ended up working in my favor, it turned out.

And now, I held an autographed advance copy of Yardley Gregson—Cash's—newest book in my hot little hands!

"Grant!" I threw my arms around him. "This is amazing! And I would *love* to keep talking to you right now, and setting up the tree and decorating it, but there's something important I have to do." I opened the cover of the book and plopped down on the bottom step of our house's staircase, flipping pages to find Chapter One.

"Roxanna!" Grant wedged himself onto the step beside me. "What are you doing? Are you reading it *right now?*"

"Fine." I grinned and closed the book. "Besides, I have something incredibly important to give you, as well." Maybe even more important than a signed advance copy of the latest Yardley Gregson.

He didn't budge, though, or respond. He wore a faraway look, so I rested my head against his shoulder. My gift could hold off for another few minutes while Grant held my hand.

"I saw you playing snowball catch with Dasher when I drove up." Grant squeezed my hand.

"He loves it." Dasher and I played catch a lot.

"Honestly? I love it too." Grant pulled me to his side. "Wanna hear a secret?"

"Sure." I wanted to hear anything and everything Grant had to say. Nerdy or flirty or noble or hilarious. His words were my soul's favorite food.

"When I first met you, I had this weird experience. I had a vision of you and Dasher playing snowball catch. It was Christmas."

"Really?"

"Uh-huh. And today, that vision came true."

He'd never told me this before, but as he did so now, I could hear a tenderness in his tone. This meant a lot to him.

"Do you want to go play now, together?"

"Sitting here is too nice."

True, except that I was a box of nerves. "Can I give you my anniversary and Christmas gift?" I had thought I could wait, but I was ready to explode.

"First, I have one more gift for you." He looked at the time on his phone. "It should be arriving any second."

"Another one? But it's not even Christmas yet." And I was dying to give him my gift. I was about ready to pop out of my skin, in fact. "Will there be anything left for Christmas morning?"

"I just got a text. They're almost here."

"Who's almost here?"

"Wait here a second." He jumped up and ran to the end of our driveway. A truck pulled up and a window rolled down. There were indistinct voices, and then the rear cab door opened, and out jumped an animal.

My breath caught in my throat. Was it? Could it be?

A white dog with a curled tail, dark eyes, and a big smile bounded toward me. I rose slowly to my feet.

"Yeti?" My voice came out a whisper. "Yeti!" I shouted. My heart stopped. That dog wasn't just any dog, not just any Samoyed. I threw open my arms, running down the steps toward the beautiful dog.

Yeti practically tackled me, licking my face. He barked once, and smiled even wider.

"Yeti!" I hugged him, rubbed his thick white fur, and buried my face in his neck. "Where have you been? How did you get here?" I looked up at Grant. "How did you find him?"

"I had to hunt far and wide, but I found him."

"This is amazing. Oh, Grant!" I should've hugged my husband, but I was busy loving on my long-lost dog. "He hasn't forgotten me." My cheeks were wet with tears. "I can't believe it. Was it hard to find him?"

"Believe me, it's been a hunt of many months. Since he's registered, I was able to track him down. Just this past month, his owners had a dramatic change of life circumstances, and they needed to re-home him. I pounced, and that was them, dropping him off. They already said their goodbyes."

"How sad for them, but how happy for me."

"It's happy for everyone."

"Grant, you're the best." I hugged Yeti, and then I got up and hugged Grant, while Yeti and Dasher eagerly greeted each other. "Do you think he and Dasher will get along?"

"I don't know. Let's find out." Grant bent down and made a snowball, and so did I. "One, two, three."

We lobbed the snowballs at the same time, and both dogs went after them. Then, they basically frolicked in the snowdrift, barking and rolling, and having the best time.

"This—wow. Thank you." I kissed Grant, and we sat back down on the top step and watched the dogs frolic in the snow. "This is a really happy Christmas gift!"

"I love you, Roxanna."

"All right, now for my gift." My hand shook. It seemed impossible to top the return of my lost Yeti, but this did qualify, actually.

"But," he said, "shouldn't I wait and get it during our anniversary dinner of Hawaiian Ham Sliders at Freya's shop?" He raised his brows. "I called ahead and asked her to brush on extra butter. My mom loves them, as you know."

Wait? It couldn't. Not this gift. "Well, my dad is coming by in an hour." He'd been released early from his sentence for good behavior. It had happened thanks to Thorn Atkins—unfortunately for my ego, but fortunately for Dad. "I think you'll want this before he comes."

"All right, but then can we play some more catch?" Grant patted Dasher on the head. Dasher was going crazy, as always. "I can't keep Dasher's energy in check much longer."

Well, Grant hadn't kept me in check very well, either, as it turned out. I handed him the gift-wrapped tube that I pulled from my coat pocket. I'd wrapped it quickly when I realized he'd return soon from picking up the Christmas tree. I'd probably be shocking him, but better now than on Christmas morning, depending on how he took it.

"What is this?" He shook the cylinder. "It feels like a paper towel roll."

"Yep."

"With a pencil inside? Did you get me one of those cool retractable pencils I've been wanting? They're good in the lab ..." He stopped short when he emptied the contents of the roll into his hand. "This is a—"

"Uh-huh." I braced myself for what he'd say next after he really looked at the plastic stick with the pink indicator in the window.

"It's a—and there are two lines." His voice cracked a little. "We're? Dasher is going to be a big brother?"

In the book, the Rygraff Queen wept when she told Captain Vartigan about his impending parenthood.

Turned out, it happened in my real life, too. I swiped at the tears wetting my cheeks. "And Yeti, too. Are you ... happy?"

"Roxanna!" He scooped me up. My long hair flew in a perfect arc as he spun me in a circle—the type of arc Domingo would have dreamed of capturing on film. "And to think—I actually expected a beloved dog and signed copy of a sci-fi novel would be the best gifts this Christmas!"

He kissed me fiercely, like he was ready for battle, but I kissed him softly, like I was ready for bed. He soon came around to my way of celebrating the best Christmas gift ever.

Dasher had to wait to play snowball catch.

196

Epilogue

Cody Haught

"Well, Dr. Haught, if I were you, I'd be flattered." Jasher handed me a large manila envelope as we walked down the hallway of the Mendon Regional Medical Center on our way to the mandatory staff meeting. "You made Dr. December."

"What are you talking about?" I opened the clasp and shook out the document inside. A glossy calendar fell out. "A gift?" Early for Christmas, but still. "Nice."

"I'd say it's more naughty than nice." He took and flipped open the calendar, thumbing past the months featuring doctors from other hospitals.

"It's called *Photoshop*." Someone had taken a shirtless photo snapped of me at last summer's hospital staff waterskiing barbecue at Newton Dam and added a Santa hat.

At least the prankster hadn't pegged me for Dr. November. That chucklehead ended up with a fan of turkey feathers around his head. Merry Christmas to me.

"I feel so objectified." I closed the calendar and dropped it in a trash can as we passed.

"Sure, you do." Jasher's wife, Sage, the hospital's anesthetist, snort-laughed. "You'd better talk to the hospital administrator and lodge a complaint."

"I totally would"—I pulled the door to the conference room wide—"if Mendon Regional *had* a hospital administrator, that is." Our last one had skipped town with zero warning, and the hospital had been a rudderless ship since Labor Day.

"Oh, didn't you hear?" Sage entered while I held the door for her.

From inside, holiday scents wafted from the refreshments table. A little early, but I'd take maple cinnamon baked goods any time of year.

"Hear what?" I followed her and Jasher over and the three of us bellied up to the buffet of fresh, hot cinnamon rolls, cookies, and brownies from the amazing cafeteria. It was the only reason any of us showed up to these pointless staff meetings lately.

"We're getting some leadership. Finally."

"Who?" I asked, but before Sage could answer, we got interrupted.

"Hey, Dr. Haught." That nurse with the snug scrubs and fake nails sidled up to me. "How's general surgery these days? Need anything sanitized?"

"Uh …" I edged away from her.

"I hope you get the holiday surprise." So she was the culprit who'd submitted my photo to the joke doctor calendar. Great.

"Looks like they're starting. Bye." I made a break for an open chair between Sage and Jasher, where Nurse Nails couldn't ambush me. If I wasn't careful, she'd do that awkward thing of walking her highly decorated fingernails up my arm again.

I sat down fast.

"There are other seats, Cody. Seats *not* right between me and my lovely wife." Jasher elbowed me hard.

"I need backup." I aimed a thumb at Nurse Nails. "She's on the hunt." I took one of Jasher's cookies. He'd piled up a half dozen.

"Hey." He grabbed it back before I could chomp a bite. "It's not my fault the nursing staff voted you hottest bachelor doc and *saved the best for last.*"

"What's that supposed to mean?" I took the cookie back from his pile and bit into it. Mmm, chocolate chip with pecans. My favorite.

Sage reached across me and took a cookie, too. "That was the caption beneath the photo of you, Dr. December." She had a snicker at my expense. "Don't make my husband feel bad about not getting selected. He gets *every* doctor-of-the-month on *my* calendar."

"Puppy love." Jasher made love-eyes at his wife, and I should've swapped seats so they could sit together, but Nurse Nails was giving me a hungry stare. "They all want you because they can't have you. That's your problem," Jasher said through a mouthful of cookie.

"Hello. They want me because I'm Cody Haught." I blew on my knuckles and rubbed them on the shoulder of my lab coat. But he was right. Not interested in a commitment, I was Lobo, the lone wolf. "What were you saying about a hospital administrator? Did they choose someone?"

"Yup." Sage pointed. "My best friend's younger cousin, so I know her a little from back in the day. Do you know her?"

"Know who?"

But just then, a woman stepped out from behind Dr. McGreeley, the other surgeon, who'd had her cornered near the whiteboard at the front of the conference room.

I choked on my own breath. "Olivia?" My heart stopped and restarted and stopped again, like it needed a pacemaker's zap.

"You do know her." Sage said this nonchalantly, as though she hadn't just thrown a javelin that had lodged in the spokes of my mountain bike and thrown me over the handlebars into the dirt. "Yeah, Olivia Olsen. I never thought she'd come back to Mendon."

Me, neither. If I'd known, I never would've spent time in Wilder River. I would've beelined it straight to Mendon so as not to miss a possible second of Olivia Olsen.

My lips tingled, and I reached up and slapped them to stop the sensation. But when I moved my hand, it started again—and for a moment, I shot down some kind of dark tunnel into the past, where we were both sixteen again, with bad hair and worse fashion, working in the Mendon High School drama club for the production of *The Christmas Music Man*. She was gorgeous, while I was a puddle of hormones and pure nerditude. Tech crew. Nobody. While she was this ethereal, angelic goddess of beauty.

"You all right, buddy?" Jasher slapped me hard on the back. "You having a stroke? Do I need to call a doctor?"

"Very funny." I closed my carp-like mouth. "We were in a play together."

"You?" Jasher spluttered. "In a play?"

"Not by choice. The drama teacher, Ms. Frindle"—an extra-artsy version of Ms. Frizzle that no Mendon High student ever forgot—"threw me in as lead at the last second, since I was the only one tall enough to wear the costume."

Sage nodded. "I heard about that."

"You did?" Oh, geez. I'd hoped no one had heard about it. But this was Mendon—quintessential small town. "I bet you never thought anyone could forget so much so fast."

I'd massively botched the lines. But how could I not? I never envisioned anything but serving on the lighting crew—when *the* Gregory Maltin failed to show up for the one-and-only performance, and at the last minute I got shoved into the spotlight and told I'd better exhibit onstage chemistry with *Olivia Olsen*.

Well, there'd been chemistry, all right. Like enough for a toxic cleanup from the school's entire science lab. And apparently no one ever forgot it.

Certainly not me.

"You remember, Jasher." Sage took another of his cookies. "The holiday hubbub when the two costars of the school play got too kissy-faced, and the principal had to personally go shut the curtains?" She took a bite. "Legendary."

Jasher's chin went up. "That was you?" He held up a fist to bump.

He dropped it in his lap when I didn't return it because just then, Olivia stepped out from behind someone else who'd cornered her—

nope, McGreeley again, on the prowl as always—and the spotlight landed on her.

Okay, not a *real* spotlight, but she did step directly beneath the beam of one of the room's can lighting's rays. Her hair shone, her face absolutely beautiful. My brain's angels broke into a perfectly harmonious choir—*aaah!*

Someone from the hospital board introduced her while I rested on the table, chin on my hand, propped on my elbow. Speaking of puppy love.

"Everyone, please welcome our new hospital administrator, Olivia Olsen." The board member stepped aside and beckoned Olivia to take the head of the table.

I clapped more enthusiastically than was warranted. Doofus alert. It drew a few stares. She could still bring out my inner dweeb.

Cool it, man. But how could I when Olivia Olsen had descended back into my life?

We'd be *working* together.

I'd get to see her *all the time.* My cardiovascular system roared with approval.

"Thanks, everyone." She smiled. Oh, I knew that smile.

"Hi, there. As the chairman said, I'm Olivia Olsen. Originally from here—although, I've been gone for quite a few years. My mom and brothers and their families are all here. Mendon has always been home in my heart."

Cool. I always said that wherever you lived in seventh grade was where you thought of as home for the rest of your life. Point of fact, Olivia had sat next to me in seventh grade science, Mr. Polson's class. Boring stuff, but I spent the whole second half of the year studying Olivia—while she diligently took notes on everything from bacteria to geological formations. *Of course.* Because she was Olivia. Funny, it had taken me until the second year of college to figure out that note-taking in class wasn't just for the Olivias of this world.

At the front of the hospital conference room, Olivia continued,

"I'm looking forward to working with each of you and to getting this already great hospital running like an even tighter ship." She offered her support to all of us and then stepped back while the next board member made announcements about the upcoming holidays.

I got distracted by a text from a consulting doctor I knew in medical school about a diagnosis. It sucked me in momentarily, and I missed the announcements. They were always about personal leave, and I always took holiday shifts. *Dad and Mom wouldn't want to see me there anyway.*

I texted the doctor back, and then I leaned back and watched Olivia again. She was looking down at a file. Studious, as always.

Ahh, yeah. Smartest girl in school, the sole woman I might consider altering my *not interested in commitment* status for—even though back when I knew her, I never would have been on her radar for any reason, let alone a commitment. She'd been so far out of my league I couldn't have seen her with a deep-space telescope.

One kiss on the stage. That's all we'd had in common.

The truth was, the play might be her last memory of Mendon. She'd up and moved right after that night.

Why? I wondered. No one had ever said.

My spine tingled, unsettling me. I shook it off. But I gazed at her again, checking to make sure my mouth quit hanging open this time.

Wow, she looked good. Mighty good. I devoured her with my eyes. Was I objectifying her? Possibly a little, but I also knew enough about her other qualities to know that the best things about her just happened to come in very attractive wrapping.

The board member wrapped up. Blessedly. Short meeting—best kind at a hospital, where we actually had a lot of time-sensitive tasks.

"Stop salivating. It's undignified." Jasher handed me a napkin, pretending to wipe my chin with it. "Just go up and talk to her. The meeting's over."

"Maybe I will." I totally would, and she'd see the not-sixteen-anymore version of me. How would she react? Impressed, I hoped. I wasn't exactly being voted least desirable doctor at Mendon Regional these days. I pushed my hair back from my forehead and squared my shoulders. *Watch out for Dr. December.* Oh, great. Doofus alert.

Doofus or not, now was my chance. I straightened my lab coat and stethoscope and sailed through the crowd to go talk with her. They parted like the Red Sea.

"Hi, Olivia." I gave her my best drama club smile—the one that Ms. Frindle, drama teacher and director, had hinted was why she'd chosen me as fill-in for that milquetoast Gregory Maltin. It hadn't just been I was the same height as Mr. Drama Club and fit the male lead's costume. "Long time."

Should I go in for the hug, or just keep it light and professional? I extended my hand to shake, deciding just to leave it in her court to decide what level of *old-friend affection* was right for us.

Us. I liked that word. Well, at least I liked the idea of getting a second shot at that kiss of hers—to see whether my teenage hormones had invented the whole thing, or whether she was actually my kryptonite and I needed her in my life.

"Oh." She frowned, looking down at my hand like it was covered in something nasty. "It's you." She glanced at my nametag and her frown grew even deeper. "You're a doctor?"

"Surgeon." That got the women's attention every time. I'd only been a full-fledged med-surge doctor for less than a year, but it'd done wonders for my cred anytime I'd met my mom's friends' single nieces, and so forth. Their eyes always lit up, or dilated, or whatever.

I waited for the standard reaction from Olivia. Wait for it, wait for it … nothing.

Well, she was an administrator. A young one. She was around doctors all the time, including dudes like McGreeley, so the novelty of meeting a surgeon had probably worn off. Plus, she couldn't exactly be seen flirting with the staff. It wouldn't be professional. If there's one thing I should've expected from Olivia Olsen, it was pure professionalism. It had been her defining trait, long before she'd become anything but a student.

"What medical school admitted you?"

What a way to phrase it. "Uh, USC?" The Keck School of Medicine was well-known and respected.

"Okay." She picked up her clipboard. "I guess I'll be seeing you." She didn't make it sound like that was a good thing. More like ipecac than sugar. She headed for the door.

What the heck? I gaped after her. Rejected? So confusing.

Jasher sauntered up beside me and guffawed. "That was entertaining." Somehow, Jasher had scored another stack of holiday cookies. He took a huge bite, which he talked through. "Crash and burn. Your explosion on impact ought to have melted her ice-queen status, since not even action-film director Michael Bay could create a firebomb that intense."

"Ice queen? No way." I knew better. She was nice. Well, if you lived up to her standards, which few did, but I'd raised mine significantly since we'd last interacted. Hadn't I? "Definitely not frigid. And I'll prove it to you."

"Oh, yeah?" Jasher and I were the last two people left in the room. "How?"

"I'll get her to kiss me." Rash promise! But also, it came straight from my heart, oddly.

Jasher laughed, spraying crumbs. "I saw how she looked at you. Like yesterday's Filet O' Fish. Good luck, buddy."

The intercom called Jasher to a patient's room, so he didn't stick around to hear my Foolproof Plan for Chill Eradication, but I had one. I'd get Olivia to warm up to me, to like me, even, and before Christmas, at that.

If that worked, I would know whether she still possessed the deadliest kiss of my life. The one that had ruined all other kisses ever since.

Or I can verify I was just a teen crushing on the dream girl, and that I blew the whole thing out of proportion, then I can finally move on

from being Lobo.
   Get past Olivia.

Continue reading <u>*Starlight Haven*</u> next, and laugh and cry with Cody and his long-lost crush, Olivia, his kiss in the spotlight that never faded away.

Bonus Recipe: World's Easiest Pumpkin Cookies

These come straight from Jennifer's kitchen. She's been making this recipe for 20+ years for her children, who are big fans of pumpkin spice.

1 box spice cake mix, any brand
1 15-oz can pumpkin (not pumpkin pie mix, just the pumpkin)
1 bag semi-sweet chocolate mini-chips

Combine all three ingredients until no powder from the cake mix remains. Do not over-mix! Drop onto cookie sheet, smallish of equal size to make about 24 per cookie sheet. Bake at 400° for 18-20 minutes, depending on your oven, or until centers are no longer wet. Watch for burning on the bottoms. Cool and eat up the warm, spicy deliciousness! To double the batch, use two boxes of cake mix and the larger (29-oz) can of pumpkin.

A Note on the Text

The bees and spring water in this story are fictional. There is no Apis polaris bee in Greenland or the arctic that makes honey, just bumblebees called Bombus polaris. They do pollinate, but they don't make honey, unfortunately.

If you would like to know more about shampoo production, there are some excellent internet articles. One I found and loved was: How Products Are Made: Shampoo. I didn't try to be a stickler about shampoo production in this book, as I thought it would distract from the main reason we love to read romances—the deep emotional connection between the destined true loves. In other words, the *romance*.

Christmas House Romance Series

The Christmas Cookie House
The Sleigh Bells Chalet
The Holiday Hunting Lodge
The Peppermint Drop Inn
The Candy Cane Cottage
The Hot Chocolate Shop
Starlight Haven
Yuletide Manor

All books this series of clean Christmas romances celebrate family, tradition, Christmas, belief, and love. They are all standalone romances, but they do connect in the small town world and can be best enjoyed in a "loop." Book 1 leads to book 2, and so on, and at the end, book 8 loops back to book 1, with recurring characters. In other words, a reader can start with any book, read the subsequent book, and then complete the loop.

Thank you for reading the Christmas House Romances. To join Jennifer's fun, effervescent newsletter—which contains a lot more *letter* than *news*—visit her website to sign up.

About the Author

J ennifer Griffith is the *USA Today* bestselling author of over forty novels and novellas. Two of her novels have received the Swoony Award for best secular romance novel of the year. She lives in Arizona with her husband, who is a judge and her muse. They are the parents of five children, which makes everyday life a romantic comedy. Connect with Jennifer via her website at authorjennifergriffith.com, where you can sign up for her newsletter to receive exclusive content and notices of new releases.

Made in the USA
Middletown, DE
13 December 2024

66893576R00121